AV

CROW MC #6

BROTHERHOOD & FAMILY BEFORE ALL

By
Michelle Dups

MICHELLE DUPS

Author: Michelle Dups
Cover Design: Joelee Creative of Indiepremades
Editor: Shelby Limon at Bookworm Edits

DEDICATIONS

This book is dedicated to my husband.
For always putting me first.

List of English Words

Twatwaffle – an idiot – general insult

Yum Yums - It's basically a deep-fried croissant, drenched in icing. They are so delicious.

Backpack – not the school kind. This is a woman that is not an Old Lady, Wife or female relative that rides on the back of a bike with a member.

Trackies/Trackie bottoms – Sweatpants

Trainers – sneakers/running shoes

Twatbastard – combination of twat and bastard

Contents

List of Characters

CROW MC

ORIGINALS - RETIRED

ALAN CROW (SHEP) m. KATE CROW

Children: KANE (REAPER) AVYANNA (AVY)

ROBERT DAVIES (DOG) m. MAGGIE DAVIES

Children: LIAM (DRACO) MILO (ONYX) IRISH TWINS

BELLAMY (BELLA)

THEO WRIGHT (THOR)

Children: MARCUS (ROGUE) BELLONA (NONI)

JACOB OWENS (GUNNY) (First wife deceased) p. BEVERLY

Children: DRAKE (DRAGON) Adopted: ALEC

JONES - DECEASED

ROMAN - DECEASED

CROW MC

1st GENERATION – ORIGINALS

KANE CROW (REAPER) **PRESIDENT** m. ABBY CROW

Children: SAM, BEN, BREN, ELLIE, KJ

LIAM DAVIES (DRACO) **VP** m. MOLLY DAVIES

Children: SOPHIE

MILO DAVIES (ONYX) **SGT AT ARMS** m. ANDREA (REA) DAVIES

Children: MILA, BOBBY

MARCUS WRIGHT (ROGUE) **ROAD CAPTAIN** m. JULIA WRIGHT

Children: ROMAN & ROSIE (Adopted)

DRAKE OWENS (DRAGON) **TREASURER** m. CALLY OWENS

AVYANNA CROW (AVY) **m.** HAWK

Children: KALEB (Adopted), Katie, Drew & Yanna (Avyanna)

BELLONA WRIGHT (NONI)

BELLAMY DAVIES (BELLA)

CROW MC

NEW BROTHERS

KEVIN LAWLESS (HAWK) **ENFORCER m.** AVYANNA CROW (AVY)

ALAN GOODE (NAVY) **ENFORCER**

AVY

SAMUEL ADAMS (BULL) **MEDIC**

WILLIAM ADAMS (SKINNY) – TECH/IT

TRISTAN JOHNSON (BLAZE)

ANDREW SMITH (BOND)

AMUN JONES   (CAIRO)

OTHER CHARACTERS

LEE MASTERS – GYM OWNER

CARLY MASTERS – GRANDDAUGHTER

WARREN, DEB, DAVID, JULIAN WALKER – JULIA'S BROTHER & FAMILY

BEAU TEMPLE

BOOKER TEMPLE

BRICE TEMPLE

MAYA LANCASTER

Children: JACKSON & EMMA LANCASTER

RAVEN - TATTOO ARTIS WITH HAWK

KELLY - RECEPTIONIST FOR HAWK

O'SHEA'S

OLD MAN O'SHEA (COLM) – NONI'S EX-FATHER-IN-LAW

RHETT - NONI'S EX-HUSBAND (IN PRISON)

LIAM

JOHNNY

ADAM

ANDY (YOUNGEST BROTHER SENT TO IRELAND TO FAMILY)

MC OWNED BUSINESSES

TRICKSTER CAFE

CROW INVESTMENTS

STICKY TRICKY BAKERY

CORVUS PUB

CROW GARAGE

CRAWAN GYM

RAVEN ROOST CAMPSITE

AVY AND HAWK'S SONGS

To Love Somebody by The Bee Gees

To Build Something by Malted Milk

CHAPTER 1

HAWK

Late January 2004
Corvus Pub, Feannag Village
New Forest

Avy was in her happy place, behind the bar in the pub that she ran for the MC. My eyes hadn't left her since I arrived earlier this evening. They never really did when I was in her presence. In a few short months, it would be nearly a year since I'd first laid eyes on her. And I was close to making her completely mine. I still couldn't believe I was lucky enough to go home with her every night.

I hadn't been looking or interested in a relationship when I'd arrived at the Crows. I'd come out of a very toxic one that had sent me travelling throughout Europe trying to run from the sick feeling of betrayal it had left me with.

How life changed in the blink of an eye; a few years ago, I'd been planning on marrying my long-term girlfriend as soon as I left the military. We'd been together for nearly eight years by that time, having met in our early twenties. Our relationship hadn't been perfect; we'd fought, mostly about how much money she spent on what I thought were unnecessary expenses. But I'd loved her, or I thought I had. Now I knew different. What I'd felt for my ex wasn't love, not like the love I felt for Avy. But while we'd been together, I'd been faithful. We'd made plans, bought a house, everything that went with a serious relationship. Or so I thought at the time.

Except fate stepped in. There had been a mess up with my release dates and I'd ended up getting released earlier than expected. I'd rushed home, not telling her I was coming early. I was in such a hurry to see her. Rachel, the woman that I was meant to be spending the rest of my life with.

The taxi had dropped me off and I'd been

surprised to see her car parked in front of the house. I'd thought that she'd be at work. She worked as a personal assistant for some company director and had done so for nearly four years.

Unlocking the door, I had been about to call out when I'd heard them. Clenching my hands, I'd taken a deep breath, and had quietly put my duffle bag down. Silently I'd walked up the stairs to our bedroom already knowing what I was going to find, but I wanted to see it with my own eyes. Taking my phone out, I got ready to take photographic evidence of her infidelity. I knew the pictures may not be clear, and I wouldn't know if they would be any good until I got to a computer to have a look at them. I knew Rachel well and if I didn't have some form of proof proving that she'd cheated on me, she'd make my life hell to get what she could out of me.

Opening the door, I expected to find her boss. I certainly wasn't expecting to find the person that I did ploughing into Rachel in long hard thrusts. The betrayal I felt when I recognised the back of the person by the tattoo that was on his shoulder. A tattoo I'd inked myself.

The person pumping in and out of my girlfriend was none other than my brother. The brother that was married with two children, who'd promised he'd keep an eye on my girlfriend while I was away. Well, he'd certainly done that and more, considering the swell of her stomach. It was the click of my phone taking a photo that alerted them they weren't alone.

I didn't even feel bad that he'd had to stop mid thrust.

Bending, I picked his pants up from the floor and threw them at him.

"Get out," I growled softly.

"Kevin, what are you doing home?" Rachel whispered in a panicked tone.

My brother chose that moment to speak. "Look, Kev," he said placatingly, holding up his hand.

I turned to him, disgust clear in my face as I pointed a finger at Rachel's clearly pregnant belly, "Is that yours?"

Shamefaced, he nodded before saying quietly, "Yeah."

I was fuming. How I kept control to this day, I have no idea. I wanted to kill him. My own flesh and blood. The betrayal cut deep.

"And Mel, the kids?"

"She left me, took the kids back up north to her family."

"So what Mike, you thought you'd just move into my house? The house I paid for and continue to pay for. Fuck my girlfriend, live here free and I'd not have anything to say about it," I yelled at him.

Rachel made the mistake of speaking. "Kevin, you need to calm down."

Turning to her, I took a deep breath and breathed slowly out, then pointing an angry finger at her, I sneered, "And you! My fucking brother, Rachel. Of all people, you pick my brother to betray me with. Not only that, but you're also having his baby. What, didn't you think I'd notice? I've not been home for sixteen months. There's no way you could have passed this baby off as mine."

Rachel lifted her chin at me, saying defiantly, "I wasn't going to. Mike and I are together now. I was waiting for you to get home to tell you."

I let out a bark of angry laughter at her words, "Really, well consider me told. Now, pack your shit up and get out."

She let out a shocked gasp, "But this is my house, you can't kick me out."

"No Rachel, this is my house. It's in my name and I pay the bills for it, which means you're squatting."

Turning to my brother, I informed him, "You and your bitch have twenty-four hours to get out of my house. If you're not out, I'll get the police involved and have you evicted from the premises. Am I clear?"

Mike nodded; he knew me well enough to know

that I was done messing around. "Yeah, you're clear. We'll be out. We can go to my flat."

At Rachel's gasp of disgust, I figured his flat wasn't up to her standard of living arrangements. I didn't give a fuck. I wanted them out of my house.

Turning, I stormed out of the room, slamming the door on the way out. Rachel immediately started to shout at Mike, and her high-pitched shriek made my decision all the easier. I was thrilled she was out of my life.

It took me a week to get Rachel out of the house. When she was finally out, I walked around and realised that I couldn't stay here, not after what they had done. Every time I walked into the main bedroom, all I saw was them. I didn't really care much that Rachel had been unfaithful. I think I'd always known in the back of my mind she'd be unfaithful. But the betrayal of my brother, that I was struggling to get over.

In the end, I'd found an estate agent and put it on the market. Once it sold, I took the majority of the sale and invested it, keeping a bit back for myself. I bought a bike and travelled for the next year. All over the UK and then into Europe, I was contemplating selling my bike and travelling to the US and then onto Australia when Bull had called to tell me about Crow MC. I'd been intrigued by the offer. I'd known Dragon and Rogue, although not well, I knew they were good guys. I'd tentatively agreed to meet them and see if it was something that I wanted to get involved with.

I didn't know at the time it would change the entire trajectory and what I wanted to do with my life. It made me realise that I'd been missing the feeling of brotherhood and family. After Mike's betrayal, I'd steered clear of any family functions. Not that there were many after my parents passed away within three months of each other a year ago. It had hit my parents hard what he'd done. I'd kept in contact with them, mostly by phone. I'd stopped in and seen Mel, my sister-in-law, and while she was bitter about what Mike had done, she'd had longer to get over it. I'd spent a weekend with them re-connecting with my niece and nephew. I'd met Mel's new man, and he'd seemed decent enough and treated the kids well. That was all that mattered to me. I'd left them, but not before reminding them they could call me at any time should they need me. I wasn't expecting a call, though; they were happy and getting on with their lives.

I'd met up with Bull, his brother Skinny and a few younger guys that had been in Skinny's unit. We'd made the trek from Manchester to the New Forest. The younger guys were excited, but Bull and I were a bit sceptical. Along the way, we'd picked up Navy. He'd been the only one from my old unit I kept in contact with. I'd called him to let him know of the offer, and Navy being Navy had decided it would suit him, so he came along for the ride to meet the brotherhood.

We'd been warned that their women were part of the MC, and if this was an issue for us, then this offer was one we best refuse. None of us were bothered by it. I'd served with women and knew they often saw things that we missed. I'd also had my arse saved more than a few times by our second sniper team and she'd been female. So, yeah, I had nothing against women being in the MC or in Church with us.

We'd pulled in and had immediately been met by what, at the time, seemed like a huge amount of people. I'd soon realised there weren't that many; they were just very loud and happy to see us.

The back door of the main house had opened, and I'd looked up, and then there she was. The quiet within all that chaos. She stood at the back door of the manor house with a smile of amusement on her face as she watched everyone. Her long dark hair was pulled back from her face in a ponytail. She'd been wearing a green T-shirt that hugged her breasts and dipped in at her waist, her lush thighs were encased in a tight-fitting pair of jeans, and on her feet, she wore comfortable looking well-worn boots. She wasn't tall, probably around five-foot-two, with curves in all the right places. She fit my five-foot-eleven height just right. I couldn't see what colour her eyes were from here, but I couldn't wait to get a closer look to see.

I'd stopped in front of her as Reaper took us around to make introductions, and if someone had told me that the world would stop when I'd meet the woman meant for me, I'd have laughed at them. But that's what it felt like. The world came to a stop; all the noise and confusion around us disappeared when she turned her piercing blue eyes on me. In that moment, it felt like she saw everything and understood everything about me without me having to say a single word. Our gazes locked and held and were only pulled apart when Reaper said something to Avy, and she turned her gaze to him as she listened to what he was asking of her. But not before she smiled at me and whispered, "Lovely to meet you, Hawk."

Her attention was taken up by getting us settled in the cottages and ensuring that everyone had what they needed.

I bided my time and while I was doing that, I noticed that Avy was the one they all turned to when something needed to be done. If it came to the MC, then Reaper handled it but anything else Avy handled. And she did so with grace and beauty, but I had to wonder if she ever said no. She'd stop what she was doing and help whoever asked even if it meant her more urgent jobs had to be put on hold. Avy did all this and never once complained. Often, I could see she was exhausted, but she'd just take a deep breath and soldier on until she'd done everything that had to be done.

I'd realised early on that if I wanted to spend time with this woman and get to know her, I'd have to make the time. I started to help her where I could, initially to get to know her better. Then it morphed into me helping to take some of the burden from her as she didn't have a lot of spare time to herself with all that she did for everyone, plus running the pub.

The change in our relationship had been gradual. We spent a lot of time together and we both felt the chemistry. I already knew that this was home. Part of it was the brotherhood – I'd missed having brothers at my back. And part of it was the woman who, since I had met her, had been at the forefront of my mind all day, every day.

I'm not sure what it was that made Avy make the first move, but that night is forever ingrained in memory.

I'd watched as the woman of my dreams closed up the pub. It was late. I waited on my bike, alert for any trouble as Avy set the last of the locks on the back door, before zipping up her jacket and taking her helmet from me when I held it out to her.

Avy Crow, she was the epitome of beauty and was good down to her soul. And I knew she was mine from the moment our eyes had met.

Once she had her helmet on and her jacket fastened, she swung onto the back of my bike with ease and familiarity. I knew both she and Noni could ride and had their own bikes, but they were both just as happy to ride as passengers.

Pulling out onto the road, I took the long way home, not just so that we could unwind but also because it meant I had Avy to myself for a bit longer.

Eventually we'd come up to the gates that Crow

Manor sat behind. I pulled up and waited as Cairo, who had guard duty in the guard hut, opened the gates. Giving him a chin lift as I drove through and into the garage where the bikes were housed out of the elements.

Holding my hand out, I helped Avy dismount before walking my bike back into its space.

Removing my helmet, my eyes had caught hers as I'd lifted my head. She'd been watching me and there was no way I could stop myself from not taking what was offered in her eyes.

Dismounting, my eyes never leaving hers, I'd walked up to her, wrapped an arm around her waist and pulled her against my chest. Avy lifted her head, her lip caught between her teeth as she looked at me from under her lashes.

Gently, with my thumb, I'd pulled her lip from her teeth and lowered my head to lick my tongue gently across her lips. Lips that parted at my touch, drawing her tighter to me, I pressed my lips to hers, my tongue entwining with hers as she moaned softly into my mouth as she wrapped a leg around my hips, pressing into my hardness.

"Hawk, if you don't take me somewhere soon, I'm going to jump your bones in the garage and I won't care a bit who sees us," Avy muttered against my *lips.*

I'd growled. Nobody was seeing her except me. Bending, I picked her up and took her to my cottage. That night, my fate was sealed; I'd make her mine completely as soon as I could.

At first it hadn't been hard, especially when Reaper had seen where my interest lay and had made me Avy's protection during our fight with the ACES.

That conversation was one I could have done without, but I understood where he was coming from. If Avy had been my sister, I'd have wanted to know what my intentions were too. I'd been clear that I thought his sister was mine, but I was taking it slowly for both our sakes.

Our relationship had been a quiet one without all the drama and danger that had surrounded the other couples. I, for one, was glad of it. I wanted Avy to be safe and loved not worrying about threats and stalkers.

In October, she'd asked me to move in with her permanently as we mostly slept in her wing anyway. I'd happily agreed and moved, freeing up my cottage for someone else if it was needed.

In November, I'd asked her to marry me, my entire being had relaxed when I'd slipped both my ring and her cut on her that now showed that she was my Old Lady. It wasn't something I'd ever thought I'd have or even want again.

We hadn't planned a wedding yet, and I was impatient to get started on that, but something always seemed to come up and take Avy's attention away from our plans. With that thought in mind, I sent a text out to Kate, Maggie, and Noni. Avy's mum, aunt, and best friend asking them to make some time for me in their schedules in the next few days.

A glass of Coke was put down on the bar in front of me and I looked up to see Avy watching me, her head tilted slightly, with a smile on her face. "You look very serious. Is everything okay?" she asked, nodding at the phone in my hand.

Leaning over the bar, I threaded my hand in her hair, pulling her closer and laid a kiss on her lips. "It's all good, Sweets, just the brotherhood checking in."

"Okay," Avy smiles at me, not asking further questions, "I'm nearly done here. Barry is going to close tonight. Do you fancy going for a ride before we head home?"

It was the first dry day we'd had in weeks, and while it was freezing, I hadn't been able to resist riding the bike out today.

"Not too a long one though, it's too cold for you to be on the bike for long. But yeah, we can take the longer way back home," I agreed, knowing the long way only added an extra ten minutes to the ride.

Avy grinned in delight. Standing on the step behind the bar, she reached over and pecked a quick kiss to my lips, saying, "Give me ten minutes and we can go."

It was more like twenty minutes, but we'd got our ride in, although we were both freezing by the time we'd arrived home. I'd hurried her up the stairs and into our room. It hadn't taken long for me to warm us both back up.

CHAPTER 2

AVY

I'd caught Hawk watching me tonight with a contemplative look on his face and wondered what he was thinking. Our romance had been a quiet one compared to the others, but I was happy for that. I wasn't a drama driven woman and could do without all the drama that had followed the other couples. I was happy with my man and the life we were building, although it was slower than I would like.

I knew Hawk wanted to get married sooner rather than later, but I'd been struggling to find the time with all the new businesses opening, running the pub and all the new babies set to arrive in the next few months.

Hawk's Tattoos had opened, and he was just as busy as me. Although he was far better at making time for us to spend together than I was. I felt awful that he was the one always having to make allowances. I sometimes wondered if he'd get fed up with my time always being taken from him. So far, he hadn't complained about it, and I know he did what he could to help and ease my stress. It's how we had ended up spending so much time together, although he'd later admitted he'd initially done it to get to know me. I'd found it sweet. And hot. I'd never been anyone's priority before, and I found it a heady experience.

I'd started to make changes in my life when we'd moved in together in October. For one, I'd started to encourage the family to sort their own business problems out and had started to say no if I felt they didn't really need me. And the second thing I'd done was I'd hired a day manager and a night manager at the pub. That had freed me from some of the responsibility. My team knew where I was if they needed me. So far, it seems to be working. It had taken me a while, but I'd finally found staff that were good fits for the pub. My day manager was a friend of the family, Keith, who'd been made redundant and had not been able to find work as he was in his late fifties. While his background was in engineering, he hadn't wanted the stress of travelling for work and had tried to find work in the towns just out of our village, but there hadn't been anything in his field. He'd been happy to learn the roles of running the pub as my manager and he didn't care that he'd be working for a woman. *'Yeah, I still had to put up with that.'* Once he got his feet under him, the pub ran like clockwork during the day, and I only had to cover for him on his days off.

My night manager, Barry, had found me by wandering into the pub with a backpack, looking for something to eat and drink. We'd got to talking; he was from Scotland and had been backpacking around Europe and was now making his way around the UK but had run short of funds. I'd had Skinny do a background check and had offered him the flat upstairs and a job. He'd been quick to make me understand it was only temporary. I'd asked him to give me two years because by then Booker would be eighteen and I could start to train him. I'd told Barry he could still travel as long as he gave me a week's notice to fill his shift. That way, he'd earn money and have a base to keep his stuff in.

We'd shaken on it, and he'd moved in. So far, it was working out. He said he wouldn't start to travel again until the spring, so we'd sat down and made a plan that we were both happy with. Having two managers meant that I had free time to spend with Hawk which made us both happy campers.

Grabbing a Coke, I walked over to Hawk, who was looking at his phone with a serious expression on his face and I wondered what had happened now. Thankfully, it had been nothing to worry about. I'd persuaded him to go for a ride. I knew it was cold, but there was nothing like the wind beating at you and the nip of the cold to make you feel alive. Plus, the side benefit of us both being freezing was that we'd warmed each other up when we got home.

And if there was one thing my man was good at, it was warming me up!

CHAPTER 3

HAWK

A few days later, I walked into the café to find it bustling with customers. Maggie caught my eye and tilted her head towards the family table at the back of the café. Lifting my chin at her in acknowledgement, I walked past the serving counter and to the table, sitting down as I waited for Maggie, Noni, and Kate to join me. It wasn't long before Noni was slipping into a seat opposite me with a grin on her face. "Hey, Hawk, this is very cloak and dagger."

I returned her smile with an amused grin but didn't say anything as Kate had just walked in. Seeing that we were already seated, she walked towards us with a smile on her face. Kate was close to sixty and was gorgeous. She had long blonde hair that she wore swept back from her face in a bun thing. I could picture Avy in thirty years' time looking exactly like her except for the blonde hair.

Bending, she pressed a kiss to my cheek in

greeting, "Sorry," she muttered, wiping what I figured was a lipstick stain off my cheek with her thumb. Grumbling about a new lipstick that left stains everywhere.

"Don't worry, Kate," I responded with a smile before standing so I could pull out a chair for her to sit. Seeing Maggie approach with a full tray of food and tea, I waited for her and helped her with the tray before pulling a chair out for her as well.

"Thanks, love," Maggie smiled at me as she sat.

We waited for her to greet everyone and make sure we all had a cup of tea or coffee depending on what our preferences were.

Once we were all settled, Kate looked at me, "So, son-in-law-to-be, what's going on, and why the secrecy?"

Taking a deep breath, I laid it all out, "I want to get married sooner rather than later and Avy hasn't got the time to set anything up. I want to take the stress away from her and do it for her, but I can't do it by myself."

Opening the notebook, I'd laid on the table with my list of everything that needed to be done, "So far this is what I've organised. I have the date and I've booked the vicar. I've booked and arranged delivery of a massive marquee, and chairs and tables, the same company also has heaters so we won't be cold as the date I've picked is in the middle of February so as long as it doesn't snow or storm, we should be okay."

"I've checked with Reaper about what I would like to do as I wanted to check that it would be okay to have the wedding at the clubhouse."

"I've also spoken to Johnny about doing the food so that Maggie doesn't have to do anything and can enjoy herself without worrying about feeding everyone."

"Johnny will also provide the disco for the evening. Drinks we can serve from the bar at the clubhouse. Is there anything I've forgotten when it comes to the comfort of our guests?"

The silence from the three of them was deafening, so deafening that it grabbed my attention, and I lifted my head from my notes to find them all staring at me with wide eyes and open mouths.

Snapping her mouth closed, Kate was the first to recover, "Well, okay then. First, I want to say thank you. Thank you for looking out for my girl and putting her first. You're right, she doesn't have enough time and don't think I haven't noticed everything you do to ease her responsibilities. You have most of it sorted so what do you need from us and what date did you choose?"

Smiling at Kate, I replied, "I chose the sixteenth of February, which is my birthday." Shrugging my shoulders, I continued a little sheepishly, "I know, but that way I figure I'll never forget our anniversary."

Noni is the first to let out a snort of laughter, followed by Maggie and Kate, and I can't help but grin at them.

Once they had themselves under control, wiping tears from their eyes at my reasoning.

"Okay," Maggie states, "I can't think of anything else you'll need other than tablecloths, decorations, and flowers. Unless the company supplying the marquee have the tablecloths. Lay it out for us, what else do you need? We only have just short of three weeks to get everything in place."

Looking back at my list I reply, "The marquee company can supply white tablecloths which I've ordered, but I wasn't sure on what colours to get for the table runners and chair covers,

I'm hoping you will know. I also wasn't sure on what flowers for the bouquets and for the tables because I don't really know what Avy would like. I know her favourite colour but wasn't sure if she'd want that for her wedding."

"I figured you ladies would know best on what to get. We also need dresses for Noni, Bren, and Ellie. And Avy will need a dress, but I'm not sure how to go about getting her one without giving the surprise away or how to get her to the wedding."

"I'm impressed," Noni smirks at me, "once this is over, you could make a second career out of event planning."

"F…" I caught myself before letting out an F-bomb as there was a family with children next to us. "Nope, this sh…I mean, stuff is stressful."

Noni giggled at my attempts at not swearing while getting my point across, while Maggie and Kate just shook their heads at me with a smile.

"So, ladies, what do you think? Can we do this?" I queried.

The three of them look at each other before nodding.

"Yeah, we can do this," Noni confirms. "Ask the marquee company if they have purple table runners and seat covers as that's Avy's favourite colour and if not that, then a dark pink. Once you know that, we'll be able to arrange bouquets and dresses."

"If you let me know as soon as you hear back, I'll sort the flowers, bouquets, and decorations." Maggie declares, "I know what Avy will like."

Kate and Noni nod in agreement and I mark the flowers off my list and add Maggie's name next to them.

"Noni and I can sort the dresses for all of them. Avy has a certain style and I know we'll find a dress that she'll love. We'll have to get Abby involved for the girl's dresses though. As to how to get her there, I think a spa break starting on Friday and back Saturday in time for the wedding. We can take the dresses and everything with us and get ready at the hotel, hair, make-up the lot," Kate declares with a determined glint in her eye. Turning back to me, she says, "You'll have to make sure her managers are aware of what's happening so that they can cover the pub, or this will never work."

I nod in agreement, "I will. I have a meeting with them tomorrow morning while Avy is with Molly at the brewery trying out a new beer."

"Just one other thing," Maggie states, looking at Kate, "only you and Noni go on the spa break. I'll stay here and help set up the marquee, flowers, and tables. That way it's less stressful for Hawk. It's his day too and you want to be able to enjoy it and not worry about decorating or table placements. Saying that, do you have a guest list?"

"There's no-one from my side as my parents have passed on, but this is the list I've made of who I think should be invited. You can go through it and let me know. I need to get the invites out within the next few days though."

"Let me see," Kate grabs the list from me and scans down it before passing to Maggie, who does the same thing and then onto Noni, who has a quick look before giving it back to me with a nod.

"Looks like everyone who should be invited has been," Noni comments.

"Fantastic," Kate whoops excitedly, throwing her arms around my neck and hugging me. "I'm so excited! My baby is getting married. And she picked herself a great man. I'm so relieved that Kane and Avy chose well. I was worried that I'd not like my kids' spouses, but they have chosen well."

Returning her hug, I pushed away the feeling of sadness that my parents weren't around to see me get married. It didn't last long with Noni and Maggie joining me in the hug. Not sure what we must have looked like to the customers hugging in the middle of the café like we were, but I found I didn't care. The hug settled something in me that I hadn't realised I was missing. The love of family.

CHAPTER 4

AVY

Hawk was hiding something from me, and I had a feeling my mother and Noni were in on it. I'd tried, but I couldn't get a straight answer out of any of them. I can't lie – it was pissing me off, not knowing what was going on. I was so used to everyone always telling me everything that not knowing something was grinding on my last nerve. If it wasn't for the fact that I knew my family wouldn't do anything to hurt me, I may have been worried about all the secrecy.

I walked into the clubhouse for our weekly business meeting, and the women were all sitting or standing around the bar waiting. They immediately all stopped talking as soon as I walked in.

Standing in the doorway, my hands on my hips and my eyes narrowed to slits as I looked at them. It wasn't long before Noni started to squirm. My eyes narrowed further when I saw Mum grab hold of Noni's hand, whispering,

"Stay strong."

I'd wanted to laugh at the comment because if anyone was going to crack it would be Noni. We didn't keep anything from each other. Ever!

I would have stood there for as long as it took for her to break, but my arsehole brother had shouted out, breaking our staring contest.

"Close the bloody door, Avs, it's fucking freezing."

Turning my glare to him, I saw he was grinning. I knew then the whole MC was in on whatever was going on. He would know that Noni would struggle to hold out on me which is probably why I'd not been able to get her on her own the last week.

Muttering under my breath about interfering brothers, I turned to close the door only to find Hawk in the doorway, reaching for me. Sweeping me up in his arms, he laid a hot and heavy kiss on my lips, then kicked the door shut behind him.

My irritation was forgotten once his arms surrounded me and his lips were on mine. My entire body relaxed as his familiar scent surrounded me. Breaking our kiss at the hoots and catcalls coming from the peanut gallery behind us, I squealed and laughed as he buried his freezing cold face in my neck, pressing his lips just behind my ear.

"Hi, Sweets, why are you glaring at Noni?"

"Because you're all keeping secrets from me and I don't like it," I pouted at him. "Are you going to tell me what's going on? I promise to reward you."

He grinned at my attempt at bribery. "Nope, it's a surprise, one I hope you'll love. I'll be giving you the first part of it tonight."

I huffed out an irritated breath and my hands were back on my hips as I glared at him, "Hawk, telling me we're going to have sex tonight is not a surprise."

My voice must have been louder than I intended it because there were bursts of laughter from behind me along with groans from what I assumed was my dad and Reaper. My man, on the other hand, was nearly bent over double with laughter. I glared at him until he stood up, wiping a hand under his eyes, his face alight with mirth. "I wasn't talking about sex, Sweets, although it's nice to know I'm getting lucky tonight." There was another loud groan from behind me. Turning my head, I looked over my shoulder to see my dad with his head in his hands shaking his head and Reaper looking a little green at Hawk's words.

I just shook my head and rolled my eyes at them in disgust. I mean, what did they think we did in my wing every night? Play canasta!

"Hawk, son, I don't need to hear what you do to my baby girl. As far as I'm concerned, she's pure as the driven snow."

Noni let out a loud snort and started laughing at Dad's comment which set the rest of the women off.

I shot them a finger over my shoulder and turned my gaze back to my man who was still looking way too amused for my liking.

"Well, what is it?" I demanded.

"Patience, Sweets, you'll see soon; it's not time yet. I'll tell you after the meeting."

"Fine," I grumbled at him, "but I'm not waiting for more than a minute after the meeting."

He smirked at me but agreed, "I promise you'll know right after the meeting."

Just then Reaper let out a piercing whistle to get us all up and moving into Church before he walked to the door where we kept all the computers and monitoring equipment.

Last year, Dragon had had Julia's brother build it as there was sometimes sensitive information showing on the screens. It was mostly Skinny's domain, but we'd all had a turn on them when he got hurt from the fire that had burnt down a barn at Molly's place.

It wasn't my favourite job, I'd found it boring, and I'd especially not liked learning about all the places the couples in this club had sex in. I could have done with never seeing that ever again.

Skinny walked out with his dog Cinder at his side. The only time she ever left it was when she played with Ellie and Mila. Otherwise, as far as she was concerned Skinny was her human, and she wasn't keen on sharing him, either. She'd made that clear when a woman at the park in December hadn't taken no for an answer. We'd taken the kids for a walk through the Christmas lights the council had set up in the park. A woman had come up and started flirting, we could all see that Skinny wasn't interested but he'd been too polite to say anything, then she'd made the fatal error of touching him, the growl from Cinder had her squealing like she'd been attacked but as she'd had her working dog vest on nothing had happened other than the woman had been cautioned about approaching people that had working animals.

The way she'd huffed and flung her hair over her shoulders before stomping away in her high-heeled boots towards her friends, only to slip on a patch of ice, had had us chuckling in amusement. She'd been caught by Cally, who'd helped her until she was steady. The woman had pulled her arm from Cally and continued to stomp away without a thank you.

"Wow," Cally said, shaking her head in disbelief as her gaze followed the woman before she'd turned back to us, "Rude, huh. Dodged a bullet there, Skinny."

This had caused another bout of hilarity from our group. It had ended up being a great evening, and we'd not had any further issues. It hadn't really come as a surprise to us that as we were leaving, we found the same woman in an argument with another woman and being shouted at for hitting on her man.

I'd just shaken my head, wondering what on earth made some women behave this way. Her friends had been standing a little way away, looking bored. That would have never happened in our family.

Our women would have all piled into the fight if it was justified, not that we'd have hit on a man that wasn't interested or clearly there with someone in the first place. I guess it took all to make the world go round.

Walking into the meeting room, we waited for Reaper to start the meeting once everyone was situated around the table. I'd emailed Skinny the financials earlier, and he'd set them up to show on the screen we had set up at the front of Church for just this reason. It made it easier for everyone to see what was happening in our individual businesses. The only one not involved in an MC business was Mum, but that was because she'd been working at the local estate agents since she was eighteen and didn't see any reason to leave a job she loved.

Standing up when Reaper nodded at me to take over, I went through everything, including the marketing plans we'd put in place for each business. It was something I'd been trying to get started for a long time, and now that Bev was helping at the garage, we were seeing the results from all the businesses.

So far, all the businesses were doing well, very well, in fact. Hence the surprise and delighted shouts coming from everyone around the table when I told them what their cut of the profits would be this month.

It would only be getting better, especially with the addition of the campsite. It looked like it would be finished in time for peak camping season, and we'd started advertising for it already. Noni had been handling the bookings, but we'd sent out an advertisement for a camp manager and we were sifting through the CVs to find someone that would fit in with the rest of us. We were getting there, and I thought we'd have someone hired by the end of the month.

Once Reaper released us from the meeting, we all congregated at the bar for a quick drink before carrying on with whatever we had individually planned for the evening.

I plonked my butt on a bar stool and turned to my man, demanding, "Well, what's the big secret?"

Hawk shook his head at me with a smile at my impatience before reaching into his pocket and pulling out an email and handing it to me. Skimming my eyes down the words, I realised I was looking at details for booking for a spa break for this Friday, my mum's name and Noni's were included on it.

"Oh, Hawk, this was the secret?"

He nodded, "Yep, and it's been hard to keep that from you. We had to keep Noni away from you as much as we could because she warned us she wouldn't be able to keep it a secret. And, before you start worrying about the pub I've spoken to both Keith and Barry, they will run the pub just fine from Friday through to Monday."

My brow wrinkled in confusion as I looked at the dates in my hand the booking showed Friday and Saturday. "Why until Monday?" I queried.

Hawk grinned at me and whispered in my ear, "Because I have plans for you the rest of the weekend as you'll only be celebrating half my birthday with me on Saturday."

I instantly felt guilty, "Oh, Hawk no, we can change the booking."

Hawk pressed a finger to my lips, "Hush, I arranged this, remember. You work hard and while I know we said we wouldn't bother with Valentine's Day, I wanted to do something for you and I know that this is something you will enjoy, plus it works out for me, too. The brothers and I are going out to the O'Shea's Saturday morning for some target practice. I promise it's all good," he assured me.

"As long as you're sure," I confirmed again.

"I am," he said pressing a kiss to my lips before continuing, "now go before your girl has an aneurism from trying to hold her excitement in."

I laughed but slid off my chair and walked to where Noni was bouncing from foot to foot in excitement.

Laughing as she wrapped her arms around me, squeezing me tight, with a soft, "You're a lucky girl, he's a wonderful man. Hold on as tight as you can to him."

I squeezed her tighter to me. I think I was the only one who realised that Noni wasn't ever going to be over Rhett. I wished that she could let him go, but I also understood how hard it was for her. Choices had been made, and she'd not been consulted. It had hurt her badly, so badly that for a long time I wondered if we'd lose her. But she'd rallied, and while she wasn't back to her normal self, I'd take this one over what she'd been like two years ago.

"I will, my beautiful sister, I promise I'll hold on tight," I promised, kissing her cheek and hugging her tighter. I didn't let go until she finally pushed away and wiped a tear from her cheek. Before she turned and walked to the door and out of the clubhouse. From the corner of my eye, I noticed Bull watching her with a sad look in his eyes before his attention was drawn away by something Navy said.

Walking back to Hawk, I pushed under his arm and burrowed into his side, needing the contact. He didn't stop the conversation he was having with Rogue about where he and Julia could go for the Easter Holidays, just made room for me and pulled me close.

CHAPTER 5

HAWK

Finishing up on my last client for the day, I cashed him out. Business was good and had really started to pick up. I knew before long I'd have to look for another artist to join me and I really needed a receptionist so that I wasn't constantly being pulled away while I was with a client. Making a mental note to speak to Bella or Avy about getting an advert set up so I could advertise the positions.

I was exhausted but happy. Planning this wedding was hard work, but I knew that if I wanted us to move forward with our lives, I would have to step up. Avy didn't have the time, and I understood that, so it was up to me to get us to where I wanted us to be.

The plus to all this planning was that I was able to spend time getting to know some of the best women other than my own mother I'd ever known. They were not only hard-working, but they were also hilarious when you got them all together. What had started out as just myself, Noni, Kate, and Maggie now included all the Crow women. I'd been worried that someone would let something slip, but so far no one had said anything.

Avy knew something was up and had been trying to get Noni alone all week, but we'd managed to keep them apart to make it easier on Noni. I knew that Avy and Noni were close but hadn't realised just how close they were. They didn't keep any secrets from each other. At all!!

I'd found this out one night when Noni had asked me out of the blue if having my dick pierced was worth the pain. The expression on my face had them both falling over with laughter.

"Babe, really?" I'd muttered at Avy, who'd just shrugged and replied, "I warned you; I don't keep secrets from my sister."

And they didn't, so we kept Noni busy with projects away from the house and the pub.

But we were nearing the end of the planning, everything was set and paid for just waiting for delivery this Saturday. I was giving Avy the spa break information tonight, and they'd leave Friday morning. I couldn't wait to make her mine. The only thing not arranged was a honeymoon, but hopefully we could book that together, preferably somewhere hot with a pool. It would be good to spend time together, just the two of us. The plus would be Avy in a bikini. Because my woman was hot, but when she was in a bikini she was beyond hot, although her dressed up in a killer dress and shoes was a close second.

With that thought in mind, I finished up, switched off the lights, set the alarm and locked up. As I was walking towards my bike, I noted that the gym was still lit up and saw Carly at the front desk chatting with a client, Ben, and Brice next to her, keeping her company.

Deciding to check on them before I left, I jogged over the road and opened the door. Ben noticed me straight away and tilted his chin at me in greeting. I waited until Carly had finished booking the client in for their next session before speaking. Once the client had left, I leant against the checking-in desk. The three of them were a solid team, and I wondered if any of the other MC members realised where this was going.

Carly smiled at me as she finished up entering details into the computer. "Everything okay,

Hawk?"

I nodded before replying, "Yeah, doll. Just checking in before I head home for the meeting. Everything good here?"

They all nodded, but it was Ben who replied, "It's all good, Hawk. We'll lock up and be home just after nine."

My eyes roamed around the gym, noting who was here. Alec was working out in the back, although I think he was flirting more than working out. Booker was in the ring with Beau. Sam, Bren, and Bella were on the treadmills. It made sense that they were all here, they seemed to do most things together.

"How are you getting home?" I asked, "Do we need to come back for you?"

Ben shook his head, "Nah, the Temples will take Carly home and Bella will drive us home now that she's passed her test," he assured me.

As they were all set, I nodded my head, tapped a hand on the desk and said goodnight before leaving. Jogging back to my bike, I fitted my helmet to my head and swung my leg over my bike and pulled out onto the road leading home. Passing the pub on the way out of the village, it looked like it was busy already, considering it was still only early evening.

Parking my bike in the garage, I noted that I was the last one to arrive and hurriedly removed my helmet before making tracks to the clubhouse knowing they would all be waiting for me.

I'd arrived just as Reaper shouted at Avy to close the door, swinging her up in my arms and laid a hot and heavy kiss to her lips. My world stopped and the stress of the day melted from me as soon as I had her wrapped in my arms. It was the hooting and hollering that had me lifting my lips from hers, otherwise I'd have been quite happy to keep them there. I buried my cold face in her neck and pressed a kiss there, making Avy squeal at the cold.

It wasn't long before Reaper had us in Church going over how the businesses were doing. I brought up that I needed to add to my staff and Avy made a note of it and I knew my woman would get it sorted.

It was good to see that all the businesses were doing better, including the garage now that Bev had taken over the office, payments were being made on the regular instead of us having to chase for money. Leaving Gunny, Alec, Cairo, and Bond to the mechanics.

Reaper turned to Avy, "Do you want to give us a breakdown of our earnings this month, Avs?"

Avy stood and walked to the front where the projector sat and spoke to Skinny. He nodded, and the next slide went up.

"Okay, so as you already know, the businesses are doing well. The garage is now earning what it should be, thanks to Bev's hard work getting all the late payments in."

The shouts of congratulations to Bev echoed loud around the room making Bev blush and laugh. Gunny looked proud and pressed a kiss to the back of her hand.

Avy waited with a smile on her face until we'd all settled back down. "You should be proud, Bev, it was a shit show down there. Noni and I gave up trying to sort it, but there wasn't enough time in the day, so thank you. And the rest of these yahoos are going to thank you even more when they see how much their cut will be this month."

I grinned at my woman's words. I'd seen the projections the night before and she wasn't wrong, the brotherhood was going to be fucking ecstatic with their cut.

Avy had the next slide up showing the

breakdown we had each earned from each business and it was nothing to sniff at. There was silence as the amounts shown on the board hit them. Both Reaper and I grinned wide at the cheer that sounded out. "That's fucking awesome," Cairo shouted out, slapping the table.

Making us laugh, because what we'd earned getting shot at was a pittance compared to what we were earning now.

I'd been giving a percentage of my earnings every month to Bella and Beau and the two of them had grown it exponentially. They were both still in college but had opened their business to family only for now. They ran it out of a small office in the back of the gym. I knew that it wouldn't be long before they'd be moving from there, but neither was ready yet to open to the public.

The figures Avy was showing would only get better once we added their business, the campsite, and Sam's woodworking business once it was solely in his hands into the fold. Abby had already added her business to the MC books.

Reaper let us out of the meeting not long after the figures were given out. To say the brothers were loud when they headed out was an understatement.

Knowing Avy was impatient, I hurried after her and handed her the spa bookings. Her happiness at going to the spa made all the hiding and secrets worthwhile. I wondered how she was going to feel on Saturday when she realised we were getting married.

We left not long after that and Avy made good on her promise that I was going to get lucky tonight. Not that it was a surprise we hadn't been able to keep our hands off each other since I'd first kissed her all those months ago.

CHAPTER 6

AVY

We'd arrived at the spa yesterday mid-morning and to say that my man hadn't spared any expense was an understatement. We'd been buffed, polished, and massaged until I was melting into the massage bed.

Although Mum and Noni had known what was coming, they hadn't expected the extras he'd organised for us, including an afternoon tea with champagne that had been delivered to our suite with a bouquet of roses for each of us.

I'd watched as over the last month Mum and Hawk had gotten closer. I knew how much he missed his parents, so I was thrilled to see them getting along. But I knew his place was solidified in her heart by the look on her face when she read whatever he'd sent her in his card that had been attached to her flowers.

"What does it say?" I asked Mum curiously. Mum smiled at me before replying with the card held against her chest next to her heart, "That's between me and Hawk, but I will say, sweetie, that you couldn't have chosen a better man."

I returned her smile, saying, "He makes all the noise stop for me when he kisses me." I didn't have to explain that to her what I meant. She'd know where I was coming from as she'd once told me that my dad calmed the chaos of life around her when he kissed her. I hadn't understood her words then, but I did now.

Turning to Noni, who was watching us, the sparkle in her eyes telling me she was happy, hiding some of the shadows of sadness that clung to them. My heart hurt for my sister who wasn't mine by blood, but she was of my heart. I wasn't sure if her heart would ever be the same as it had before Rhett. "You going to tell me what yours says?" I asked her.

She shook her head that no, she wasn't going to share with me. "I won't share, but I will say you need to hold on tight to him and not let a single day go by without letting him know you love him. Because life isn't always roses and it can throw shit at you when you least expect it. And he's one of the good ones. I know in my heart that he will always put you first over and above anything. As long as you're happy, he'll be happy." We sat there staring at each other for a short while.

I heard her words and took them as she meant them, that I had to remember not to take anything for granted because life was short and could change in the blink of an eye, as she well knew.

Seeing that I understood where she was coming from, she smiled, wiped a finger under her eyes and took a deep breath. "Well, let's eat this fantastic-looking tea, drink that champagne and then maybe go for a swim. What do you say?"

Mum and I knew Noni well, she'd said her piece and was ready to move on to the next bit, and Mum and I would let her. Grabbing the champagne, I opened it and poured our glasses. Holding mine up, I toasted, "To some of the best women I know. Thank you for always being there for me."

Clinking my glass against theirs, we drank it down before tucking into the scones, cakes, and sandwiches on the table. In the end we didn't go for a swim because there'd been a knock on the door and when we'd opened it, we'd found a waiter there with another bottle of champagne and a note from my dad.

To my Queen,

Hope you and our princesses are having a good time. Enjoy a drink on your Old Man.

All my love always,

A

xxx

Of course, we'd had to make another toast in thanks to my dad. While we didn't get sloppy drunk, we'd been very happy when we'd crawled into our bedrooms later that night.

I'd not gone to sleep straight away because when I'd phoned my man to say thank you, we'd spent another hour doing something I'd never done before. Phone sex was hot and while I came, it wasn't as satisfying as having him in my bed with me.

When I'd informed him of this, he'd laughed softly, "Tomorrow night, Sweets, I'll rock your world."

I'd giggled, still a little drunk and even more relaxed after an orgasm that while it wasn't as good as when we were in bed together was still good none the less.

"I'll hold you to that, handsome." I let out a happy sigh, still smiling as a yawn took me.

Hearing it, Hawk said, "Sleep, baby. I can't wait to have you back home tomorrow. Our bed is too empty without you."

Still smiling, knowing he'd hear it in my voice, I replied, "Night, handsome. Love you."

What I got was a deep guttural moan before he replied, "Night, baby, right back at ya," and the phone went dead. Still smiling, I snuggled down in one of the most comfortable beds I'd ever slept in and slept like a baby until I was woken up way too early by a way too chirpy Noni who looked like she hadn't had a drop to drink the night before.

Groaning loudly at her bouncing on my bed, I shoved a pillow over my head doing my best to ignore her. There was a slight throb just behind my eyes and my mouth felt like I needed to drink about a litre of water before I'd feel human again.

"Rise and shine, sister. We have a shed load to get done and not much time. I have orange juice and paracetamol ready and waiting, and breakfast is on its way."

With a heavy sigh, I removed the pillow from my head. From experience I knew I may as well give up and just do what Noni wanted. Sighing,

I turned over and looked up at my sister from another mister who was beaming happily at me from where she was sat on my thighs. Crossing my eyes and sticking my tongue out at her, I grumbled, "What the hell, Noni, why are you up so early? And what do we need to do that can't wait until later."

Leaning across me, she picked up a glass and the paracetamol, holding them out to me, "These first and then I'll fill you in. Aunt Kate will be in shortly with the breakfast."

Muttering at her, I pushed myself up in bed until I was leant against the headboard, taking the orange juice and paracetamol from Noni I downed both finishing the juice just as Mum walked in pushing a serving trolley that was filled with breakfast.

I narrowed my eyes at the both of them, they were both looking way too chipper and there was an undercurrent of excitement on their faces.

"What's going on?" I demanded.

Mum squealed and I mean literally squealed and did a little dance where she was standing by the trolley. "You're getting married today, baby."

I was shocked speechless. What were they

talking about? Pushing Noni from my legs, I swung them off the bed, "Explain!"

Mum and Noni exchanged a look, so I knew they were in on whatever was going on. I mean, how did they even know what I wanted and if it was going to be a quick registry office wedding, I wasn't going to be happy.

Placatingly, Mum held up her hands, took a deep breath and started explaining, "A few weeks ago Hawk came to us with a plan, that man wants to marry you and marry you as soon as possible."

"But he knew with all your responsibilities that you didn't have the time to plan anything, and he wanted you to have the day of your dreams with no stress. He had most of it all organised except for flowers, colours and dresses which is why he came to us."

"We knew what you would like, so we helped him with all of the stuff he wasn't sure of. But honestly, the man didn't need much help. He's bound and determined to make you his in all ways."

"And there was no way we weren't going to give him all the help he needed to make you his because," Mum paused as she looked at me her face serious, "because, baby girl, you don't let a man like him go when he's proved that you will always be his priority. All I've ever wanted for you and Kane was for you both to be happy."

"Kane, I had no worries about once he met Abby but you, I worried about. Because you work so hard all the time, always putting the club and the family before your own happiness."

"Then Hawk came along and started to take some of that responsibility from you and I watched for months as all the drama unfolded within the MC and he was there every step of the way, and I knew when he slipped that ring on your finger that finally you'd found your one and your dad and I couldn't have been happier."

"Not just because we liked him and then came to love him but also because we knew that he'd work every day to make sure you are happy. And that's all we've ever wanted for you was to be loved and happy."

At the end of her speech, I was blinking back tears. I'd not realised that my parents had ever worried about me. Getting up off the bed, I hurried to my mum and wrapped my arms around her in a hug.

"Love you, Mum," I whispered.

"Love you too, baby girl. Can't believe you're

getting married today."

I laughed softly, "Me either."

Stepping back, I wiped at my eyes, "So, are you going to show me my wedding dress?"

Noni wrapped her arms around me from behind and rocked me back and forth, "Nope, not yet, but I promise you will love it. Breakfast first, shower, hair, make-up, and your nails are already done, so we're good there, then we'll show you your dress."

Mum did another little jig making us laugh. I don't think I'd ever seen her so excited. "I promise, baby girl, you'll love your dress."

And she was right, I did, when they finally let me see it. It was perfect and fit like a dream.

My dress had long beautifully embroidered champagne coloured lace sleeves with tiny pearls sewn into the flowers, it had a deep plunging neckline that was outlined in tiny diamantes and pearls, a draped skirt that stopped just on my ankle, so it didn't trail on the floor. There was no train I was relieved to see. Under it I wore the most beautiful lingerie that Julia had sent as a present.

The hairdresser had put my hair up in intricate braids with pearls, thin ribbons, and diamantes woven through the braids. I don't know how she did it, but it was beautiful. My make-up was light with a light pink lipstick to match my nails. On my feet were a pair of butter soft cream boots with a slight heel. They matched the colour of my dress almost exactly.

Standing in front of the full-length mirror in the hotel bedroom I stared at myself, hardly believing it was me. Mum and Noni walked up behind me both looking gorgeous.

Mum had on a lilac-coloured suit, her hair and make-up had also been done as had Noni's. Noni's long hair was up the 1950s hairstyle that she favoured with Victory Rolls and a low bun at the back. She had purple flowers and diamantes woven through her hair. She was dressed in a deep purple gown that fit her curves to perfection and showcased her red hair and green eyes. It also had long sleeves and a plunging neckline and stopped just above her ankle. It was plain with no adornments. Where my dress had a wide skirt, hers was fitted. In her ears, she wore the pearl earrings her dad had bought her for her eighteenth birthday and that was it. Dropping my eyes to her feet, I saw she too was wearing new boots and hers were purple to match her dress.

"So, what do you think?" Noni asked, a little apprehensively.

Smiling wide at them both, I told them, "I love my dress. You picked well." At my reassurance, both their shoulders relaxed in relief. "And you both look beautiful."

"Oh, baby girl, so do you," Mum said emotionally as she came and stood beside me.

Turning around so I could see them, I asked, "So what's next on the agenda?"

I'd no sooner finished my sentence and there was a knock on the bedroom door. Noni opened it to the photographer who had arrived while I'd been in the shower and who had spent most of the morning taking photos of us all getting ready until I'd shooed him out so that I could get dressed.

"Ah just in time," Mum beamed. "A few more photos, then down to the limousine to take us back to the manor where you'll be married."

"What about your car?" I asked.

"Cairo came in the limousine and has already left with all our luggage back to the manor," Noni replied. "Don't worry, Avy, it's all in hand, all you have to do is get in the car to get to the manor, walk down the aisle to your man and say

I do," she grinned at me.

I grinned back at her, excitement bubbling in my belly at the thought of being Hawk's wife.

I gathered my skirt in my hand and started walking to the door, "Well then, let's get this show on the road, I have a man to make mine," I stated.

Mum and Noni laughed and followed me out, down the stairs and out the door to the limousine. I stopped and smiled when I saw that the driver was Adam O'Shea. He was in a suit and had the back door open waiting for me with a smile that widened when he saw me. "Ah, Avy, you look gorgeous. Hawk's a lucky man."

Smiling back, I took the hand that he held out to me, "Thank you, Adam, you look pretty fabulous yourself."

He grinned back at me but didn't say anything as he helped me into the car before helping Mum and Noni in. Once we were settled, he closed the doors, and we were off. I checked the time on my wristwatch and saw it was just after one in the afternoon. It would take us about forty minutes to get back to the manor if there were no issues with traffic. I was excited to see what else was in store for me. I couldn't believe that Hawk had done all this just so that I'd have one less thing to worry about. I don't think I could love the man more.

CHAPTER 7

HAWK

Surveying the massive marquee, I couldn't help but feel amazed that we'd managed to get everything done in time. The tables were set up beautifully with swathes of dark purple ribbons and draped cloths, with the same covering the chairs. The flowers had arrived and been added around the tent. We'd blown up what seemed to be thousands of balloons and twined twinkle lights through them and around the poles. Everyone had stepped up to get it all set out and ready for this afternoon. We'd been busy since six thirty this morning, and it had been organised chaos, but the marquee looked fucking awesome.

I was so fucking lucky that I had the brothers I had and the women in this MC that had stepped up big time to help me get everything organised.

We'd set the chairs up on the temporary dance floor for guests to sit on during the ceremony. Once the ceremony was done, our soon-to-beprospects would move them to the tables while we were having photos done. The O'Sheas had everything set up for the food and the music for tonight. Cairo and Bond had said they'd handle the bar in the clubhouse and pour drinks.

We'd lucked out on the weather and while it was cold, it was dry and there was no wind. The outdoor heaters had been lit, and the marquee was warming up nicely and should be good by the time the ceremony started.

I can't lie, I'd been bricking it a little this morning at what Avy would think of me steamrolling ahead and setting all this up without her input. That was until I'd received a message from her an hour ago to say she'd loved me before today but loved me even more now for doing this for her. And that she couldn't wait to be Mrs. Hawk.

I'd breathed a sigh of relief at her words. I was showered and ready to get this show on the road, I just needed my bride to arrive. I know that Adam had picked them up because he'd messaged me when he left the hotel. So, it wouldn't be long now.

I turned when I felt someone come and stand next to me and saw it was Avy's dad, Shep.

He grinned at me and squeezed my shoulder, "You ready, son?"

I nodded, "Yeah, I am. They should be here soon."

"Here," Shep handed me a shot glass filled with whiskey. Taking it, I looked at him as he studied me, his eyes serious before he said, "I've dreaded this day for years, knowing I'd be giving my baby girl away. Worried that she'd pick some arsehole that I'd hate, and I'd lose her. I can't tell you how relieved I am that she chose you. Kate and I couldn't have asked for a better man for our girl. Thank you for always making sure she's okay and for giving her this day." Tapping his glass against mine, he threw back his shot.

Joining him, I drank mine down and hissed at the burn as it went down, warming me up from the inside out. Shep took my empty glass and went to leave, but I stopped him with a hand on his arm.

"I love her, Shep, you and Kate never have to worry about me and her. I'll always put her first, same as she does for me when she needs to. Avy is one of the strongest women I know, she was raised by strong women and if we have girls, I'd hope they turn out just like her. So, I think it should be me thanking you for entrusting her to me and as we're not going anywhere, you can still kick my arse if you feel I'm not doing my job," smiling broadly at him to lighten the mood.

He chuckled, nodded, slapped my shoulder, saying over his shoulder as he walked away, "True brother, I'll be keeping an eye on you."

My phone beeped, taking it out of my pocket, I read the text from Noni.

Noni – 20 minutes out. Get people settled.

Me – Thanks.

Lifting my head from my phone to look around the crowd of people to find Reaper. Seeing him standing near the open clubhouse doors, I lifted my hand to catch his eye and tapped my watch. I walked to the front and stood near the vicar who was chatting with Dog, apparently, they'd been in the same year at school together.

"They're twenty minutes out," I told the vicar, who nodded.

"You let Reaper know?" Dog asked just as there was a loud whistle and he cringed. "Yeah, you let him know," he beamed a wide smile at me, giving my shoulder a hard clap before wandering off to go sit next to Maggie.

"Right people, let's get settled down; the bride is

nearly here. Take your seats, so we can get this show on the road," Reaper bellowed out.

Reaper joined Shep at the entrance to wait for Avy, Kate, and Noni to arrive, he'd be walking his mum to her seat. Bren and Ellie were waiting with them, both looking beautiful in cream long sleeve dresses tied at the waist with purple ribbon and purple boots to keep their feet warm. They'd been amazed when I'd asked them to be part of our day not expecting it. I'd made sure they'd got the full treatment at the hairdresser this morning. Bren had found me when they'd come back and wrapped her arms around my waist in a hug. The look on her face had been thanks enough, but she'd said it anyway. I felt sorry for Reaper because his girls were beauties, probably just as well this next baby was a boy.

Navy walked up to join me in the front as my best man. He smirked as he walked up to where I was waiting near the vicar. The man scrubbed up pretty well and if I wasn't mistaken, he'd had a haircut and beard trim by the looks of it. We weren't in suits, instead, we both wore black trousers, with black button up shirts and purple ties to match the colour scheme.

"You ready, brother?" Navy asked as he stopped next to me.

"Can't wait," I replied with a small smile.

We didn't say anything else because we'd heard the car with Avy arrive and I knew it wouldn't be long before I saw her. I shuffled a little impatiently as first Reaper, Bren, and Ellie disappeared followed by Shep out the marquee.

Five minutes later, Reaper was back in the entranceway with his mum to escort her down the aisle. Pachelbel's Canon in D Major started, and they walked down the aisle towards us, Kate was smiling big and winked at me as she took her seat. I smiled back at her before turning to watch Ellie followed by Bren walk down the aisle, Ellie throwing rose petals in front of her, a serious look on her face, making sure they were all gone by the time she got to the front. Bren showed her where to stand and they both beamed wide happy smiles at me. Then it was Noni's turn, and she was smiling hard as she walked towards us before taking up her position next to the girls.

I took a deep breath, knowing that this was it, she'd be next, and I couldn't wait. And then there she was, a gorgeous vision in cream lace, standing next to her dad, looking up at him with a smile as he said something to her. Then the music changed to the wedding march and her eyes found mine and the world fell away until it felt like it was just the two of us. I moved forward and waited until they got to me, her eyes never once wavered from mine until it was time for her dad to put her hand in mine, which he did with a smile leaning down to press a kiss to her cheek before leaving to sit next to Kate.

Leaning forward, I whispered in Avy's ear, "You look beautiful, Sweets."

She smiled happily up at me until we heard the heavy throat clearing behind us. With a last wink at my future wife, I turned us to the vicar who was waiting on us with his eyebrows raised but had a twinkle in his eyes.

"If the bride and groom are ready," he questioned with a small smile and there were a few titters of laughter from our guests.

Avy and I nodded at him that we were ready, and he started the ceremony. Because Avy hadn't known about our wedding, I'd opted for the traditional service and thirty minutes later he was declaring us husband and wife. I didn't hang around when he said I could kiss the bride. Gathering Avy into my arms, I swooped in and laid a long kiss before dipping her back over my arm at the end. Pulling her laughing back up and into my arms for the vicar to give us the go ahead to leave as a married couple. Which he did in short order.

"Ladies and gentlemen, I give you Mr. and Mrs. Kevin 'Hawk' Lawless!"

There were whistles and applause as we walked back down the aisle and out to the clubhouse to sign the wedding registry as well as have pictures taken.

Finally, Avy was wholly and completely mine in all ways.

CHAPTER 8

AVY

We were nearly at Crow Manor. I couldn't sit still, the bubbles of excitement in my belly were ready to fly, and it had nothing to do with the champagne I had just finished.

Noni had pulled her phone out about twenty minutes ago and sent a text message to I'm assuming Hawk. All I'd got was a wink and a smirk when she saw me watching.

And then Adam was driving us through the gates at the Manor, my eyes widened as we drove past the garage by the main house and onwards towards the clubhouse where there was a massive white marquee set up on the grounds adjacent to the clubhouse. I hadn't given a thought of where the actual ceremony was going to be held but obviously my man had.

Dad, Reaper, Bren, and Ellie were waiting for us at the entrance to the marquee. The girls looked gorgeous in their cream dresses and purple sashes. Bren was holding a small bouquet and Ellie was clutching the handle of a small basket. I had to chuckle when I noticed that Dad and Reaper were each holding a bouquet. I assumed one was for me and one for Noni, but that didn't mean that I wouldn't tease them about it.

Adam swung the car around and parked so that my door was right near where they were all waiting.

I smiled wide as Reaper opened the door for me, standing back out the way. Then Dad was there, and his eyes got a little misty as soon as he saw me. He held out his hand to help me out.

I stepped out of the car and straight into his arms. Inhaling his familiar smell of Old Spice and peppermint from the mints he chewed on the regular since he gave up smoking.

"Hey, Daddy."

He let out a gusty sigh and let me go, holding my hands out the side so that he could see me properly. Clearing his throat, he blinked a few times before saying huskily, "You look beautiful, baby girl. Just like your mum."

That had me tearing up, and I blinked rapidly at his words to stop them spilling over before replying with a soft, "That's the best compliment you could have given me."

"No crying," Noni informed us as she and Mum walked around from the other side of the car, where Adam had helped them out. She took her bouquet from Reaper with a grin, "Why thank you, Reap, although it suited you, you can carry it if you want."

Reaper laughed, "Shut it, trouble."

Turning to Mum, he kissed her cheek, "You look amazing, Mum."

"Thanks, son, you all clean up nicely." Turing to look at the girls who had been standing quietly waiting for us, she smiled, "Well, don't you girls look beautiful. I love your hair."

Ellie grinned and twirled so we could see the full effect, "Hawk had the lady at the hairdresser do our hair this morning and our nails," she held out her hand which had a clear coat on and made her nails shiny. I smiled as Reaper muttered about them growing up too fast. Turning my attention to my older, much quieter niece, "You look beautiful, Bren."

Bren looked at me with a small smile, happiness clear in her gaze, "Thank you, Aunt Avy and thank you for having us in your wedding."

"Well, it's the only one I plan to have, so I'm glad

I've got my favourite girls in the pictures with me," I informed her.

"Talking about pictures," Noni pointed at the photographer that I'd hardly noticed as he took pictures of us as we stood chatting. Not sure where Hawk found him, but he was good, half the time I'd forgotten he was around.

The photographer lowered his camera at her words and motioned to us, "If you could all stand together, I'll take a quick photo before you head inside," he informed us.

I took my bouquet that Reaper was holding since Dad had passed it off to him when the car pulled up.

Not long after the photographer had taken half a dozen photos moving us as he wanted us. Making Dad grumble and Mum hush him.

"Stop it, Shep, it won't be much longer."

"Sorry, Katie, I didn't sleep well last night," Dad muttered a little sheepishly wrapping an arm around her waist and pressing a kiss to her head. "You look beautiful. I missed you last night. Don't like not having you in my bed, woman. Next time I'm coming with, hate not having you to hold on to and you know how I wake up in the morning."

Reaper, Noni, and I groaned, Bren laughed softly, thankfully Ellie wasn't listening. She was more interested in what the cameraman was saying.

Mum laughed and bumped his shoulder, "Hush, Shep, little ears. I'll make it up to you."

Reaper gagged, and I was hard put not to do the same thing.

For as long as I can remember, they'd been like this. I guess it's one of the reasons both Reaper and I had waited so long to find our other halves. I'd always wanted what my parents had and with Hawk, I know I had it. It wasn't just the Crow men that knew when they'd found the one, us Crow women did too.

"All done," the photographer said and disappeared inside.

"Right then. You ready, Mum?" Reaper asked, holding out his arm for her to take.

"Ready, son," Mum replied, taking his arm but not before sending me a wink over her shoulder, "See you on the other side, baby girl."

Smiling wide, I nodded in agreement and watched as my brother escorted her into the marquee to the sound of one of my favourite bits of music, Pachelbel's Canon in D Major. Ellie, Bren, and Noni stood ready to take their places.

Dad and I chuckled as Ellie disappeared into the marquee; I could imagine the look of concentration on her face as she scattered the rose petals I'd seen in her basket. Before long, it was Noni's turn. Dad and I moved until we were just inside the marquee. My breath caught as I took in the beauty of the decorations, my favourite flowers, and colours prevalent throughout the chosen theme. The entire marquee looked fantastic.

"Ready, Avy?" Dad asked with a squeeze to the fingers of the hand I'd threaded through his arm.

Tilting my head, I smiled up at my dad, his eyes had taken on a misty look again, "So ready, Dad. Don't be sad, I'm still going to be just down the hall."

He took another deep breath before he smiled back at me, "True, baby girl, and you picked a good one."

The music changed to the wedding march, and I stepped forward, my eyes catching Hawk's as he stepped forward to wait for me. Then, as always, when I saw him, the world stilled, and the chaos subsided. He looked so good standing there waiting for me dressed in black with a deep purple tie to match our wedding colours.

The love he held in his eyes as he waited for me to reach him made me happy. I couldn't stop the smile from beaming from me. Then, there he was, taking my hand from my dad, bending he whispered in my ear that I was beautiful.

The rest of the ceremony was a bit of a blur, but I know I said all the right words because before long, the vicar was telling us it was time to kiss the bride. I was not disappointed in my first kiss as Mrs. Kevin 'Hawk' Lawless, because if there was one thing my man knew how to do, it was kiss me senseless. Dipping me over the back of his arm before pulling me back up into a standing position, I was smiling so hard my cheeks hurt.

The thrill the vicar's words sent through me as he introduced us as the married couple.

I may not have had anything to do with organising my wedding, but it was everything I could wish for. As was the wedding reception where Navy had us in stitches of laughter during his best man's speech.

We wouldn't be going on a honeymoon anytime soon with Hawk having just opened up the tattoo shop. Instead, during the father of the bride's speech, Dad had handed us an envelope from him and Mum. They'd booked us a cabin with a hot tub in the nearby town at one of the holiday parks. It was booked from tonight until mid-day Monday. I was looking forward to spending some one-on-one time with my new husband.

The party was still going strong when we left, Adam again driving us the half-hour to our destination, informing us that our bags and food were already inside and that someone would be back to pick us up on Monday.

"Thanks, Adam," I said, pressing a kiss to his cheek. He smiled, "You're welcome, Avs. Congratulations!"

"Thanks for all your help today, brother," Hawk said, giving him one of those half hugs and back slaps the men did. "And thank Liam and Johnny for all the help with the bar, food, and music."

Adam nodded in agreement, "Will do, brother. See you both next week."

He got in the car driving away, leaving us standing watching as the taillights disappeared. Once he was gone, I turned to Hawk who'd already opened the cabin door. With a wicked grin, he bent and scooped me up in his arms, making me laugh as I threw my arm around his neck.

"Welcome to our home for the next few days, Mrs. Lawless," he growled at me, his eyes heated as he kicked the door shut behind him and walked with me to the bedroom and setting me on my feet.

The air around us grew thick with hunger and anticipation. We'd not spent a night apart since we'd made our relationship official. It wasn't long before his mouth was on mine, his fingers spearing through my hair, pins flying as he hungrily attacked my mouth.

"Fuck, Sweets, I hated being away from you last night," he growled as his lips latched on to my neck.

I hummed in agreement as I pulled his shirt from his trousers so I could get my hands on his skin. His tie was long gone, impatient I ripped at his buttons, ignoring them as they pinged around the room, sighing in happiness now that I had his chest bared, pressing hungry kisses to it as I attacked the button on his trousers, feeling his cock hard and ready for me. Pulling the zipper down I wrapped my hand around his long hard length, and he gave a guttural groan as I slowly pumped him, his hands tunnelling under my skirt pulling my dress up to my waist, he stopped as his hands hit my thigh highs, muttering, "I'll enjoy these later."

Then his fingers were on my clit, pressing and circling, and I knew it wouldn't be long before I was coming. My orgasm hit me out of the blue, no warning. Suddenly, I was up against the wall, my panties in tatters on the floor and Hawk was in me. Thrusting hard into me, my back sliding up against the wall of the bedroom with every thrust as I tightened my legs around his waist pulling him deeper and deeper with every plunge until I threw my head back and shouted his name as another orgasm hit me and I came hard at the same time as I felt his warmth coat my walls.

Panting, I slowly came down, Hawk's face buried in my neck, my arms and legs wrapped around him, "Fuck, Sweets, I think I saw stars," he growled into my neck making me laugh, which then made us both moan as I pushed him out of me.

Slowly, I released my legs but kept my arms around his neck as my feet found the floor, the skirt of my dress falling back down, I whimpered at the loss of having him inside me, my whimper turned to a moan as his lips found mine.

"Love you, Avy," he whispered against my lips.

"Love you too, Hawk," I replied with a smile.

"Let's get you out of this dress, I want to see you in those tights," Hawk rumbled as he turned me around to get to the buttons on the back.

Once I was out of my wedding dress, which was left forgotten on the floor of our room as my husband proceeded to show me just how much he approved and appreciated my new lingerie.

I'd have to remember to thank Julia for her present, I thought sleepily as I drifted off to sleep, feeling sated and loved.

CHAPTER 9

HAWK

Being woken up by the smell of cooking bacon was never a bad thing. Although I was surprised that Avy was up already. I'd kept her busy until the early hours of this morning. We hadn't been able to get enough of each other. I was a lucky fucker that had a wife that was happy for me to let me love her like I needed to.

We'd always had a connection, but now that she had my name it was like I couldn't restrain myself. I already wore her name on my skin and had done since the day I'd slipped her engagement ring on her finger in October. I couldn't wait to mar my wife's virgin skin. For all that she was an MC princess, she did not have a single bit of ink on her. When I'd asked her why, she said she could never settle on anything but that she always knew that when she found the man she wanted to spend the rest of her life with, she'd have his name inked on her.

When I'd heard that I started to design the

perfect tattoo for her. I knew exactly where I'd like to put it on her but would understand if she wanted to have it somewhere else. I'd brought the design with me to show Avy, and I'd kept Monday afternoon free just for her so I could get my name on her body as soon as possible. Call me a caveman, I didn't give a fuck, I wanted to own every piece of her that I could. I'd never once felt like this in any of my previous relationships, which was one of the reasons I knew this was it for me.

From the day I'd met her, I'd wanted to have my name on her. That need had been slightly appeased when I'd seen my patch on her cut. I'd wanted my name to be blazoned across Avy's back, warning everyone that she was mine because my woman was hot as fuck but seemed oblivious to it. She had the bearing of a highborn lady, but you could tell that she would get business done if it was needed as she'd shown with Molly's situation. I loved her sense of loyalty. She was so fucking loyal to everyone, her girls, her family, the club, and now to me. If there was one thing, I would never have to worry about, it was Avy's loyalty and I hoped that she knew she'd never have that worry about me.

Getting up, I hit the bathroom and did what I needed to do before venturing naked out into the main part of the cabin, where I found Avy at the stove dressed in one of my T-shirts. She was reaching up to get something out of the cupboard when I walked in, noting that she was naked from the waist down. Instantly, I was hard; walking over to her, I pressed up against her back. Lifting her heavy hair, I kissed the nape of her neck, causing goosebumps to rise on her arms and for her to squirm and laugh softly as I pressed another kiss to her neck. Grinding my cock into her backside, I smiled as Avy pushed back against me. "Morning, Sweets," I whispered in her ear before nipping at it. Avy let out a whimper, leaning her head back against my chest, giving me further access to her. "Morning, handsome," she responded.

Pressing another kiss to her neck, my hands wandered around to the front of her body and over her breasts, tweaking her hard nipples, causing another shudder to make its way through her. Lowering my hand, I found her pussy and smiled as my fingers trailed through her wetness. Yeah, my woman was ready for me. Avy sighed softly as I ran a finger around her clit, letting out a breathy moan.

Not wanting to wait any longer, I reached over and switched the stove off. Turning my wife in my arms, I hungrily devoured her lips. Picking her up, I set her down on the kitchen's island.

"I was making you breakfast," Avy smirked seductively at me.

I winked at her, "Oh, Sweets, don't worry. You're still feeding me breakfast. You'll be my first breakfast and the bacon can be my second breakfast," I informed her. "Now, be a good girl and open those legs for me."

Avy's eyes heated at my words as she did as I asked and opened her legs for me. I hummed in appreciation as I took in her dripping pussy, pink, swollen and ready for me.

Taking her legs, I gently lifted them and set her feet on the counter, opening her up further for me. Leaning down, I breathed her in, licking at the moisture coating her thighs as an appreciative rumble came from deep within me as I breathed in her scent, "Fuck, Sweets, you smell so good." Avy gasped at my words and then hissed as I pinched her clit with my fingers, hips shifting restlessly. "Stop teasing, Hawk," she whispered, sounding a little desperate.

At her words I gave her a long lick before flicking

my tongue hard against her clit, and her hips jolted in response. Gently, I inserted a finger into her hot channel and felt the first flutters, feeling how close she was, making me wonder what she'd been thinking about while she'd been cooking. I added another finger and found the slightly rough spot inside her, rubbing up against her walls as I sucked her clit deep in my mouth before letting it go and again fluttering my tongue against her.

Avy came hard and fast with little warning and with a loud wail. I waited while she panted slightly and came down from her orgasm. She caught her breath, and I pushed for one more. "Hawk," Avy whimpered, "I need you inside me."

"You'll get me, baby, but you need to give me one more." Avy's eyes were heavy with lust. "I'm not sure I can do another one," she replied huskily.

"Just one more, Sweets, I know you can do it," I reassured her as I kept pumping my fingers slowly in and out of her. I pressed my mouth to hers and ravished her mouth with mine, our tongues twining around each other, and before long, her pussy was spasming around my fingers. I lifted her off the island before she finished; she let out a keening cry of dismay. Hurriedly, I turned her and pressed her upper body down onto the island. Lifting her hips slightly, I pressed my hard weeping cock into her softness with a grunt. Holding myself still until Avy ground herself against me and ordered huskily, "Hard, Hawk, as hard as you can."

Never let it be said that I don't listen when my lady speaks. I thrust in hard and fast just like she asked. I slipped one hand under her and strummed her clit until we both came.

Sagging against her back, I lifted her shirt and pressed a kiss to the top of her spine.

"Love you, Hawk," she mumbled her eyes shut, face relaxed. I grinned a self-satisfied smile at her relaxed state. Gently disengaging from her, picked up my very relaxed wife and took her to the bathroom to clean her up then tucked her back into bed before pulling on some underwear and going to the kitchen to finish up breakfast. We ended up eating it in bed before I dirtied her up again. We'd had a fantastic sex life before, but since I'd seen her sign her new name something had snapped in me, and she seemed hotter than ever. I wondered how long it would be before she'd let me put a baby in her belly. Until then, I'd enjoy practicing.

CHAPTER 10

AVY

It had been two weeks since my surprise wedding. I wasn't sure what it was about being married, but it seemed to set something off in Hawk. He couldn't seem to get enough of me. Not that I was complaining. We'd had a great sex life before we'd got married, but it seemed that with each little thing that further tied me to him, the hornier he got.

First it was my cut showing his name on it, then it was my engagement ring and finally our wedding. I never thought I'd say this, but my vagina needed a break. She was crying for mercy. Not that he'd ever force me, and I know that if I said something, he'd stop.

Nope, we were both just as bad as each other. My vagina wasn't listening to me needing a break … she was a hussy for his cock and always seemed to be open for business as soon as his cock was anywhere near her.

This morning I'd got up before him and told him that I had an emergency at the pub and hightailed it out of the house before he'd even thought about getting up. I was now hiding in my office, wondering if I should find an icepack to sit on. My office door opened, and I looked up in alarm and then sighed in relief as Noni popped her head around the door. She burst out laughing at the look of relief that must have shown on my face.

"What's up, Avs," she smirked at me.

"Fuck off, Noni," I grumbled at her, closing my eyes, and laying my head tiredly back on my chair.

She sniggered at me, "I thought you'd be in a better mood with the number of orgasms you've been having," she cackled.

Opening one eye I glared at her, "Why are you here? Leave me to my misery."

She laughed louder at my words, "Pussy not liking the pounding it's been getting?"

I muttered a curse word at her, rubbing my hands tiredly over my face, "That's the problem, she likes it too much and now I can barely sit in comfort. She needs a break and I'm putting her on time out. Who knew getting married would ramp up my sex life."

I glared harder at Noni, who had fallen back on the couch I had in my office, crying with laughter at my words.

When she finally stopped laughing, she wiped her eyes and grinned at me, "Just tell him. Because hussy, it's not just him, you've been just as bad, especially since he added the Property of Avy's patch to his cut. The rest of the brotherhood are muttering hard about that, especially Draco once Molly caught sight of it."

I couldn't help the smug grin that spread across my face at her words. The looks on the faces of the brotherhood when he'd shown up at Church last week with a new patch sewn on his cut had been priceless. The only ones not surprised had been Reaper and my dad, but he'd have had to ask permission from Reaper before adding it, so that was understandable.

It only made me love him more and yeah, that night it had been me that hadn't let up. I wasn't sure if my birth control was going to hold up to the amount of sex we were having. Not that it would be an issue if I did end up pregnant. It would be great if my kids grew up close with the rest of the cousins that were about ready to pop out in the next few months.

A balled-up piece of paper hit my forehead, shaking me out of my sex infused daydream. I glared at Noni, who just grinned at me unrepentantly.

"Bitch, stop daydreaming about cock and show me the tat. It must be healed enough by now," Noni demanded.

Ah, yes, the tat that Hawk had inked onto my body as soon as we were back in the village. I'd loved the design he'd shown me, and he was having a similar one done on him just as soon as he found another tattoo artist that he trusted that could blend in the tattoo of my name he already had.

Standing, I unbuttoned my jeans and pulled them down so that I could show Noni, who'd come closer to examine it. He'd placed it just above my right hip bone, it was bigger than expected and took up quite a bit of my lower belly.

"Oh wow, Avy that's beautiful and I love the words," Noni whispered as she studied it.

Hawk had designed the tattoo with a hawk in flight carrying purple peonies in its talons, the petals fluttering loose and blowing in the wind with the words *'Always Hawk's'* written in cursive amongst the blowing petals. He was having one done with similar words, although his said *'Always Avy's'* written in the ribbon tied around a bouquet of purple peonies. It was the most feminine thing he'd have on his body, and I couldn't wait to see it inked on him. He was going to have his placed on his body in the same place that he'd placed mine.

"Do you like it?" she asked, looking up at me from where she was still studying my tat.

"I love it," I assured her. "Hawk is having his completed as soon as he can get into his tattoo artist or if he can hire someone for his shop, whatever happens first."

Noni stood up and I buttoned up my jeans and sat back down. "I love this for you," Noni beamed at me with a happy smile and sat back down with a happy sigh.

"And you?" I asked her. I hadn't touched base with her for a little while, but I'd noticed that she had gotten quieter and quieter over the last few weeks.

"What about me?" she asked.

Perusing her silently with narrowed eyes, I knew when she was stalling and not wanting to answer my question.

Noni rolled her eyes at me before standing up and gathering her jacket, avoiding looking at me. "I'm fine," she muttered as she wrapped her scarf around her neck.

"Noni!"

"Honestly, Avy. I promise I'm good," Noni assured me with a smile. A smile that didn't touch her eyes.

She wasn't good, but I let it slide, knowing she'd just clam up if I continued to push her.

"Okay," I said, letting it go, "but remember I'm here for you if you ever need me."

This time the smile that she sent my way was real, "I know Avs. Love ya, chick, but I've got to get home. I promised Ellie that I would do some crafts with her when she got home from school, and I want to catch a nap first. Getting up at three in the morning is getting old."

"Noni, if you need a break, take it. We can get cover for you," I told her.

"I'm good for now, Avy, but yeah, I may take you up on the offer in the future. Let me think on it," Noni agreed as she opened the door before leaving, blowing a kiss at me and waving as she left.

I can't lie, I was a little worried about my childhood friend. She was struggling and had been for a long time. Ever since Rhett got put away and then divorced her in short order. It didn't matter that he thought he was doing her a favour by setting her free. He'd broken something in my friend, and I wasn't sure if we would ever get her back.

With a tired sigh, I sat back down, switched on my computer and got lost in spreadsheets. Spreadsheets for me were always a lot easier to understand than people.

CHAPTER 11

HAWK

"All done, man," I said, finishing up a tat on a client that I'd come in early for. And when I mean early, I mean five in the morning early.

There weren't many people I'd do this for, but Cai had been one of my first clients when I first started out over ten years ago. When I joined up, he would wait until I was home on leave. I often speculated on how he would know when I'd be home because he'd be on my doorstep the day after I got back, ready for more ink therapy.

He was running out of space for me to tat, but I'd never turn him away. Not only was he my first client, he was also a scary motherfucker.

I'm not sure if they were an MC or not as they didn't wear anything identifying them as such. I did know they were nomads, always on the move. There were four of them and I wouldn't like to be on the bad side of any of them. EVER! All of them were well over six foot five, they hardly spoke, were watchful and always in control. They reminded me a bit of Vikings from old, as they all had long hair that they kept plaited in various braids. I'd never seen them wear helmets or any other safety gear and often thought it was curious that they didn't get pulled over by police more often.

I started cleaning up as he lumbered over to the full-length mirror I'd hung on a wall to inspect his new addition.

"All good?" I queried.

Cai gave a grunt, his nearly black eyes met mine in the mirror. He nodded his head that yes, it was all good. I knew that I'd not get anymore from him, so I walked out towards the reception to take payment.

The rest of his brothers were sitting outside on their bikes, relaxed but watchful.

I'd offered to let them sit inside out of the cold, but they'd declined.

Taking the pound notes that Cai handed me to pay for his tattoo, I didn't bother to count them as I knew from past experience that he'd give me the correct amount. He'd also not book another appointment; I'd get a text when he was ready for his next one.

"Thanks," I said, bending to put the money in the lockbox that I'd take to my office and put in the safe once he'd left.

He tapped the counter twice and walked out of the door. I followed and locked the door until I'd completed my clean up. Taking the lockbox with me, I put it in the safe, switching off the lights I made sure all was secure, set the alarm and went to leave but was surprised to see that Cai and his brothers were still outside and seemed to be waiting for me.

Walking towards them, I asked, "Everything okay?"

Cai tilted his head towards one of his brothers. I frowned wondering if one of them wanted a tattoo. I'd hate to say no, but it was family breakfast at the café being it was a Sunday and it's what we did every Sunday as per Abby's orders. I'd hate to annoy my Pres's pregnant Old Lady.

The dark-haired brother held out his hand, "Silas," he introduced himself.

I shook his hand, surprised that he'd spoken never mind introduced himself. Other than Cai, I didn't know any of their names.

"Good to meet you," I responded. "What can I do

for you?"

Silas didn't say anything but seemed to be studying me and I had to wonder why. This obviously had nothing to do with a tattoo.

Silas sighed as if this was painful for him and changed his stance from looking at me to hands on his hips and lowering his head as if contemplating if he should really be doing this. Seeming to make up his mind, he looked at Cai one more time and Cai nodded at him with a chin lift as if to say *get on with it* as he threw a leg over his bike and settled down and got ready to leave.

Just as I was starting to feel the first flutters of annoyance at his procrastination, he seemed to make up his mind about something.

"My brother likes you," Silas informed me. "And he doesn't usually like anyone."

'Huh, I'd never have guessed' I thought. I wasn't sure where this conversation was going but my interest had been piqued.

"So, I'm going to go out on a limb and let you in on something because my brother trusts you," Silas continued.

Now I was intrigued, wondering where this was going.

"Okay," I agreed, "what information do you have that I need to know?"

Without any warning, he reached out and took hold of my shoulder. His hand tightened, and his eyes turned white, the words out of his mouth shook me to my core. Although it wasn't so much the words as the way he delivered them, *'Your path is diverging, should you not take the right path, your happiness will end. Learn from your light and embrace what you are being offered. Love comes in many forms.'*

He abruptly let go of me and stepped back.

His eyes returned to normal. That was seriously fucking weird. Not that I didn't believe in some people having certain abilities. I'd been in the military long enough to know that when your gut told you something was off, then something was off. And I'd lived with Ellie for nearly a year and what that little girl knew and saw firmly had me believing in weird shit.

Just never expected it to come from a giant that I didn't know except in passing. Added to the fact that I had no clue what any of it meant, other than it seemed to be a warning of sorts. I wasn't feeling happy about any of it.

"I'm not sure what any of that meant," I told

him.

"I know," he replied, "but when it starts happening, you will. I see two outcomes and the one doesn't fill me with happiness. I hope that you take the right path because if you don't, everything you are building will wither away."

"What do you mean?" I demanded.

"I can't tell you more; you need to make the decisions. I can give you some advice, though. When you are uncertain you need to trust in your wife, she'll show you the way," Silas assured me.

'What the ever-loving fuck was going to happen?'

Dropping that last bit of wisdom, he got on his bike and with chin lifts from all of them, they pulled out of the parking and onto the road, disappearing into the distance. I was stuck frozen to the pavement outside my shop, that's where Avy found me.

"Hey, babe, are you, okay?" she queried, coming to a stop next to me.

Shaking off the warning, I smiled at my wife, replying, "Yeah, Sweets. Sorry I'm running late."

"You're not late, we just weren't sure what was happening with the giants that were sitting waiting for you. It seemed serious. We could see you from the café window," Avy gestured to the windows of the café just up the road from my shop. The brotherhood was standing waiting, Bull and Navy were outside the doors as if they'd been ready for me to call them. It made me feel better that they were around after hearing the cryptic message from Silas.

I waved at them and got a chin lift in return, then they turned and entered the café. I cupped my palms around Avy's cheeks, and smiled at her, "I'm good, Sweets," I promised. "I'll tell you about it later. For now, I'm starving. Let's eat and then we'll head home and have a lazy day. Yeah?"

Avy beamed a wide smile at me, "Yeah, sounds perfect."

I should have known that it wasn't going to be as easy as that. As soon as we took our seats and started filling our plates everyone was demanding to know what the giants as they started calling the four nomads wanted.

Giving in I told them of the weird warning that Silas had given me and that I didn't have a clue what it meant. Trust Ellie to break it down for me in simple form.

"It's easy, Uncle Hawk. Something is coming, it

could be good or bad depending on how you handle it. And you need to listen to Aunt Avy and do what she says and all will be good. Don't worry, it will all be fine. We'll help," she said matter-of-factly, looking at me with clear blue eyes.

The table was silent as they looked at her. She smiled at me, "It will be fine, I promise. You just need to open your heart."

With that parting bit of insight, she casually went back to eating her breakfast obviously feeling like her job was done.

Reaper and Abby were watching their daughter. I know they worried about her. For now, she seemed fine. Abby would touch base with Ellie during the day as she usually did to make sure all was good in her daughter's world.

I'd instantly felt lighter at Ellie's words. "Whatever is coming, we'll deal with it as we usually do," Reaper confirmed with a firm stare in my direction. "Together."

I nodded in confirmation that I was hearing him loud and clear, "Together," I agreed relaxing back in my seat.

Little did I know we'd be dealing with it before the end of the day.

We'd just finished eating and had started cleaning up when a brand-new white Mercedes pulled up in front of the café.

It immediately drew our attention because it wasn't a vehicle often seen in our little village.

Then she stepped out, and I froze. *'What the ever-loving hell was she doing here.'*

She hadn't changed much in the years since I'd last laid eyes on her. She was still pretty and dressed well. She looked good just like she always had. But I also knew that inside the pretty package was a cold heart. Avy had more warmth and love in her little finger than my ex had in her entire body.

'Fuck this' I thought to myself, *'there was no way she was coming to cause issues in the life I'd built for myself.'* I understood some of what Silas' warning was all about now. I don't care what Ellie said, there was no way I was opening my heart to this bitch ever again.

Standing from my chair, I stormed out of the café towards where she was standing by her car looking up and down the street.

"Rachel, what are you doing here?"

Ignoring the way she perused me as she smiled at me in a way that she'd used to when she wanted something from me. I could now see it for what it was. Fake. Everything about her was fake. I knew this because nothing about my wife was fake. Avy was real in every way.

"Now is that anyway to greet your former fiancée," she smirked at me, then irritated me further by reaching out and running her nails down my arm. Jerking my arm away as she let out a laugh at the motion, "Looking good, Kev baby."

"What do you want?" I growled through gritted teeth.

"Straight to the point, huh. You haven't changed a bit," she sniggered. "Well then, okay, I thought I'd drop our son off with you. I've looked after him for long enough. My mother died and my new man doesn't want a snivelling kid around him."

I stared at her in shock, rage coating my next words, "Are you high?!" I exploded at her. "You and I don't have a kid together."

She shrugged carelessly, "That's not what his birth certificate says."

This woman, I couldn't believe her. I ground my back teeth, praying for patience, running my hand through my hair in agitation. "What the fuck did you do, Rachel?"

For the first time I had her full attention, and I noticed it was stuck on my wedding ring which was still bright and shiny as we'd not even been married a full month yet.

"You're married," she uttered, looking shocked.

I was fuming, if ever there was a woman I'd wanted to strangle, it was the one standing in front of me.

"Yes, I'm fucking married. Now tell me what you've done, so I can go about fixing whatever mess you and my brother have cooked up."

"Your brother," she said and looked confused for a second as if she didn't remember it was my brother's baby that had been in her belly, not mine.

"Yes, Rachel, my brother! The one who you were fucking while I was away. The one whose baby was in your belly. You do remember him?"

Dismissively, Rachel waved her hand at me, "I haven't seen Mike since before the baby was born. No idea where he's got to. I put your name on the birth certificate."

"Jesus, Rachel, what the fuck! Why?"

With another careless shrug, "I knew that Mike

was a waste of space. A good fuck, but a shit dad and that you would do better. So, I figured I'd just put you on the birth certificate. It isn't like I've hounded you for child support or anything, Kev. His being born hasn't affected you at all. I left him with my mum, but then six months ago she up and died. I don't have any room in my life for a baby, so, he's your problem now."

Rearing back in disgust at her thought process, I couldn't believe how callous she was being about her own child. But then I shouldn't be surprised. I'd seen how Reaper's kids' parents had treated them until they'd been adopted.

"You're a fucking cunt, Rachel."

"And you're being a fucking dick, Kev. It's not like he's some stranger's kid. He has your fucking blood running through his veins," Rachel glared angrily at me.

I'm not sure what she was expecting from me, but my anger and vitriol seemed to come as a surprise to her. Did she really think I was going to bend over and just take whatever she dished up to me? Her son was the reminder of the betrayal that she and my brother had laid on me. Anger and resentment bubbled up in me. I knew it was wrong, their son wasn't to blame, but I couldn't help myself.

"Look," Rachel, said running a hand down her ponytail pulling it over her shoulder. It was then I knew she wasn't as certain as she seemed. She always did this when she was nervous. "I'm away for the next three weeks. Keep him for me and I'll come pick him up when I get back. I'll put him up for adoption or something if you don't want him."

Her callous, blasé attitude toward her son made me angrier. How could she care so little for the being she'd birthed? "You're a serious piece of work, Rachel, I can't believe you."

She snorted, "You know exactly what I am, Kev. I never wanted kids. But Mike talked a big game, and I left it too late to do anything about it. Then when he was born, I was going to put him up for adoption, but Mum persuaded me to give him to her to bring up. Which was fine, except six months ago she up and died on me and now Kaleb's suddenly my problem."

"That's because he's your fucking son," I ground out in anger.

"Well, I don't want him," she snapped back at me. "Look, just meet him, take him for a few weeks and I'll sort something out when I get back, okay?"

With that she stormed back to the car, opened the back door, and said something.

I stared, shocked as a little boy toddled his way towards me. It was like looking at Mike and me in the past, the same black hair and when he looked up, I saw he had our green eyes. He was also filthy, in clothes that weren't suitable for this weather and looked like he hadn't had a good meal in months. My anger at Rachel and Mike rose again at the sight of their son and the obvious lack of care he'd had.

I knew as soon as Avy stepped out of the café. I'd heard the door open and felt her presence at my back. I'm surprised it took her so long to come out. I realised it was because she'd seen the boy in front of me. I also knew that she'd step in and take him if he had nowhere else to go. I knew my wife and her family. There was no way they'd ever let any child go without, especially if that child was tied in blood in some way.

She slipped her arm around my waist, and I relaxed now that I wasn't standing here by myself. She'd staked her claim and made it clear to Rachel by laying her hand on my chest, her new rings shiny on her ring finger. Avy quietly murmured to me, "Talk to me, handsome."

So, I filled Avy in on why Rachel was here. Not

long after that, she had my nephew in her arms, and he held on to Avy like he knew she'd be there for him always. He held on so tight I'm not sure how she was breathing, but she didn't remove his arms. She just wrapped him up tighter in her arms while walking away from us.

Issuing an order to her dad as she walked past them. No sooner had she issued her orders to Reaper and Shep about Rachel not leaving than Rachel was jumping in her car and taking off down the road before there was anyway we could stop her.

"FUCK!!!" I shouted as we watched her car disappearing out of the village.

"Calm, brother," Reaper squeezed my shoulder. "We'll get it sorted."

"She'll be back," I said. "But we need to find my brother."

"Then we'll find him," Shep reassured me. Just then, Blaze jogged back towards us carrying something. I'd not seen him leave us.

He held out a black backpack to me, "Here, I saw her throw this out of the window as she sped away."

Pulling the zip down to open the bag, inside was a change of clothing and what looked like paperwork. Taking it out, I saw it was a birth certificate and a book with his vaccination information in it. Looking at the birth certificate, I saw that she'd not lied. Under father, she'd put my name.

With a sigh, I handed it to Reaper, who raised his brows. "He's not mine, I promise," I stated.

"We know," Shep assured me. "But don't look at this as a bad thing. With your name on the certificate, it will be easier to get custody of him."

"I have to speak to Avy first."

"Hawk, if I know my daughter she's already on board. You don't have to worry about her."

"Okay," I agreed because I know he's right. But how did I explain to people that took on children not of their blood that I was struggling to accept the fact that my brother's child, who was my blood, had been dumped on me?

I felt like a dick, and I wasn't liking what I was feeling. I was an adult, and I knew that little boy had nothing to do with my brother's betrayal, but it felt like a slap in the face seeing him and how much he looked like me.

Avy and I were just starting out and now my brother's bullshit was creating issues for me again. And as usual, I'd suck it up because that's what I did.

I'd speak to Avy tonight and get her take on what we should do. Here I thought we'd managed to not have any drama clouding our relationship. Seems I was wrong.

Behind us the café door opened, and the women came out with Molly in the lead followed by Noni. I met Avy's eyes over the heads of everyone and she knew just by looking at me that I was struggling. I'd never kept her in the dark about how I felt about what my brother had done. Rachel's cheating hadn't bothered me. It had been my brother's betrayal that had cut me deep.

Our gaze was broken by Molly, who sounded put out when she muttered, "Can't believe that bitch did a runner. I was hoping to get some practice in. I'm getting rusty, not being able to have any fun."

Her grumbling broke the tension, and we laughed. "Come on, Firecracker. Let's get you home and we'll set up and throw some knives," Draco grinned at her. She smiled back at him, "Sounds like a good time to me. Anybody want to join us?"

A few of the brothers and most of the kids said they would, and I knew this was to give us some time at the main house without a crowd. I could imagine that my nephew was pretty freaked at all the people.

That they all knew instinctively what was needed and didn't make a big deal about it just went along and made it happen.

Wrapping my arms around Molly, I pressed a kiss to her temple.

"Thanks, Molls." She smiled up at me, "Anytime, Hawk. I'm learning. It's what family does."

Passing her back to Draco, who was grinning at his Firecracker with pride. I left them to walk to my wife, who was waiting for me near the door. Inside I could see Maggie sitting with Kaleb at the table and looked like she was giving him something to eat.

Pulling Avy into my arms, I relaxed as she wrapped hers around me. "How are you doing, handsome?"

"I'm not Avs."

"I know, honey. But we'll get through this, I promise."

God, I hoped so. Silas's warning was running

wild through my head, reminding me that I had to choose the right path. How did I know what the right path was though? I didn't want to lose the best thing that had happened to me and what we'd been building.

How could I ask my new wife to take on my nephew when I wasn't sure if I even wanted to?

CHAPTER 12

AVY

I watched as Hawk stormed out of the café towards the blonde standing by a new Mercedes. She was dressed in what looked like a designer outfit from top to toe in tight jeans, knee-high boots, and a plush looking coat.

Unfortunately, I also recognised her from a photo I'd found when Hawk had moved in with me. Not that he'd tried to hide the photo of her, it had been mixed with photos of his family that we'd been looking at. He'd told me straight away who she was.

There was no denying she was beautiful, the total opposite to me. She was tall, probably about five-foot-seven or eight. She had long blonde hair that she wore up in a high ponytail.

He'd never lied to me about his relationship with her, and I knew he didn't have any time for her or his brother after what they had done. Although I think he was more upset by his brother's betrayal than he was by Rachel's infidelity. He kept in touch with his ex-sister-in-law and his niece and nephew but that was it.

We all watched as he got to the front of her vehicle and confronted her. I knew her type straight away; she used her looks to get what she wanted. I shook my head as she smiled flirtatiously up at Hawk and reached out as if she was going to kiss his cheek. I snorted a laugh as he pulled back with a look of horror on his face that she'd attempted to touch him. The fake look of hurt on her face caused another snort of laughter to erupt from most of the women at the table. The men looked at us as if we were nuts, but they didn't get it. We knew manipulative when we saw it, and this bitch had it down to a T.

"Do you want to go out there?" Molly asked, looking excited. That was Molly, always ready to rumble even if she looked like she was a hundred weeks pregnant, not the five months that I knew she was.

I grinned at her but shook my head. "Not yet, let's see what she wants first. If she steps out of line, I'll go out."

Molly pouted and huffed out a sigh sheathing the knife she'd taken out when she'd asked her question. "Fine!" she grumbled, making Draco laugh and press a kiss to the side of her head.

'My man was getting annoyed' I thought as he shoved his hands into his hair and looked up at the sky. His body had gone taut with tension at something she'd said.

He shook his head as she walked away to the back of her car and opened the door. She said something to someone in the back, but we couldn't see who. I stood up so fast that my chair fell back and onto the floor with a loud crack. A little boy with a dark head of hair toddled out from behind the open door and nearly stumbled and fell. She'd not even helped him out.

My heart clenched in my chest as I watched as the small boy was revealed. He looked to be around two years old. He toddled over to stand still next to her, his face tilted to the ground. He was dressed inappropriately for this weather, not a coat or hat in sight and the clothes he was wearing looked like they were a size too small and weren't clean from what I could see even from this distance.

He lifted his little head as Hawk said something else to his ex-fiancée.

And my breath stalled in my chest because even from this distance, I could see how much he looked like my man.

"What the fuck?" I heard Reaper growl out in anger. I stormed towards the door. Behind me Reaper called out, "Avy!"

Impatiently, I turned to look at my brother over my shoulder, "What?"

"Don't go out there half cocked, you don't know what's happening. Hawk obviously didn't know about the boy."

I smiled, I got it now, my big brother was worried. Hawk and I had only just got married and now there was a strange woman here that Hawk obviously knew, and she had a baby with her that looked just like my Old Man. I could see why they were all worried.

"I know the baby isn't his, Reaper, it's his nephew. The woman is Hawk's ex, though. He doesn't keep shit from me. I know it all," leaving them with that information I pushed out the door.

Resounding sighs of relief echoed around the café at my words and I'm not sure who it was but a relieved, "Thank fuck," echoed out.

I was going to find out what she wanted and why that baby had a look on his face that no baby should ever have. As I left the café, the door slamming shut behind me, I heard Mila squeal out a laugh and wondered if this little boy had ever laughed like that.

Walking to my man, I wrapped my arm around his waist. "Talk to me, handsome," I murmured quietly to my husband.

Hawk's entire body relaxed as soon as I wrapped my arm around him. He flung his hand out at the woman who'd tensed as soon as I'd made myself know. There was no way she could miss the rings on my finger that I'd purposefully laid against Hawk's chest. I know she saw them because her nostrils flared slightly at my possessive move.

"Rachel here doesn't want to be a mother anymore and never has. She dropped him off with her mother when she left the hospital with him nearly two years ago and left him there. But her mum passed away six months ago, and nobody knows where my fucking brother is, so she thought she'd drop their son off with me, so that she can go on holiday with her sugar daddy," he ground out angrily.

Behind us the café door opened and shut again, and I knew the brotherhood felt like they'd given us enough time and were coming to see what was going on. It made me feel better knowing they were behind us.

I hummed slightly under my breath while I studied her. I'm not sure what Hawk ever saw in her other than the obvious big tits, blonde hair, and body because there was no way you could miss the cruelty in her face nor the anger in her eyes when she realised this wasn't going to be as easy as she thought.

My eyes dropped to the little boy standing quietly next to her. No two-year-old that I knew of was ever this quiet or stood this still and I couldn't help but wonder what he'd seen in his short life. My heart hurt as he lifted the most beautiful green eyes to mine. They were eyes that I saw every day when I woke up and again before I went to sleep. Eyes that looked at me with love whenever they happened to fall on me. I wanted to cry at the sadness in them. No baby should ever have such a look on their face.

My heart cracked wide open, and I knew there was no way he was going to go back with this she bitch. I got it now what Reaper and Abby meant when they said that they'd loved their adopted children on sight. Blood did not make a difference to our family. Removing my arm from around Hawk, I knelt down, holding my hands out to the little boy, saying softly, "Come here, baby."

I waited patiently as he studied me and I don't know what he saw in my face, but his little face crumpled, and tears welled in his eyes as he stumbled to me and into my arms. I picked him up and cuddled him tight into my body. He burrowed his little head into my shoulder, wrapping his arms so tight around my neck it was hard to breathe but I didn't move him, my nose did wrinkle a bit at the smell, and I wondered when she'd last bathed him. He cried but not a sound left his body and my anger rose again. There was only one way he'd learned not to make a noise when he cried.

Turning to Hawk, his eyes widened at the anger on my face when I spat out, "Do not let her leave, I'll be back in a minute."

"What the fuck, you can't hold me here," Rachel screeched from behind me as I walked away from them. I stopped by my dad and Reaper, saying fiercely, "She does not leave. Make it happen."

Getting a nod from both of them, I walked into the café hoping that the men would be able to stop her from leaving. I should have known better, though. Women like her always knew when to run.

Going to the table that held most of the women in my family, I looked at my mum and she must have seen something on my face because she stood and came to me as I shushed the little boy in my arms. Gently, I removed his arms from around my neck as I sat down with him in my lap. He still had tears streaming down his face, leaving clean tracks on his dirty cheeks.

Taking a serviette, I wet it in a glass of water and wiped at his face, cleaning him up.

"Mum, I want you to get hold of the lawyer and have him meet us in the back room of the gym with adoption paperwork. I don't have this baby's name, but I will in the next hour. You have mine and Hawk's details," I informed my mother, who nodded in agreement but still asked the question, "Are you sure this is the way you want to go?"

Pressing a kiss to the head of the little boy on my lap, I nodded, "Yeah, I'm sure."

Mum smiled, "Okay then, guess I'm a grandmother again."

"Congratulations, sweetheart," Maggie said, coming up with a piece of buttered toast and jam which she held out to the toddler on my lap. He didn't take it from her, just looked at it, then at me. At my nod, he reached out for it and devoured it, making me angry all over again. Not only was he filthy, but I also wondered when she'd last fed him. By the looks of the faces in the room, I knew they'd agree with my next questions.

"You ladies ready for some fun?"

"Hell, yeah," Molly said, getting up from her chair and waddling her way towards the door.

"Absolutely fucking ready," Julia muttered and followed Molly but not before running a gentle hand over the head of the baby that I held.

"I'm always with you," Noni agreed, standing and helped Abby up next to her, who looked over at Ellie, indecision on her face. "I've got her, Mum. You go do what you have to do," Ben assured her. Abby nodded and followed Noni outside, Beverly joining them not long after.

"Let me take him and Rea can look him over, then she can go over to the gym and make sure you haven't done any permanent damage to the cum receptacle that carried this beautiful baby," Maggie said holding out another piece of toast to him before holding her arms out to take him. Again, he stopped to look at me, but at my nod, he went to her. It seemed he instinctively knew he could trust me.

"Go," Rea shooed me, "I'll make sure he's okay then I'll be over to minimise any damage you do to the bitch."

Standing up from the chair I'd been sat in I took a step towards the door before turning to look at Aunt Maggie holding the precious baby boy, Rea, and the rest of the Crow kids, and I knew then my life would be changed forever by the trust that baby showed me. I vowed then nobody would ever hurt him again.

Unfortunately, we were too late to stop Rachel from leaving, which left me with a burning anger deep in my soul.

She did at least do the decent thing and throw a bag out with his paperwork which we'd need, because there was no way he was going back with her. I don't care if she did come back in three weeks to get him. My girls and I'd take care of her then. I didn't think she would, though. She wasn't stupid, and she'd seen how Kaleb had clung to me. She also knew Hawk and what type of person he was.

I knew Hawk would struggle with taking on Kaleb, but I knew he'd do the right thing in the end. I never doubted it.

CHAPTER 13

HAWK

I was struggling.

Kaleb had been with us for just over a month.

It was getting harder and harder for me to pretend everything was good. It wasn't that Kaleb was a bad kid. He wasn't. If anything, he was too quiet. He rarely smiled. If he did, it was usually at Avy. Not once since he'd been with us had I heard him laugh. He was so serious, and I felt in my gut that as young as he was, he knew how I felt about him. As soon as I walked into a room that he was in, it's as if he tried to get smaller, so I didn't notice him. Not that any of this was his fault. It wasn't. I took full responsibility for it all.

Avy had moved him into the room next to ours and the longer he was with us, the more the room was looking like something a little boy would love.

I knew I had to get over this because it wasn't

fair on him or on Avy who already loved him. I could tell just by how she lit up as soon as she saw him. I guess some part of me wished he was ours.

I'd known that as soon as Rachel had left, we'd not see her again. We'd tracked her trail, and we knew she'd left the country the same day she'd dumped him on us. We knew this because we'd found the man she was dating, and I use the term dating loosely. She was fucking him, plain and simple. What we'd found about him didn't fill me with joy. He was a man that liked variety and he went through the women like they were water.

Skinny had had to dig deep to find out how his money was made. While he owned a well-known nightclub in London that was a legitimate business, he made a fair amount moving drugs through it. But his most profitable venture was the escort service he ran for high end rollers. And I think we all agreed that the escort service he ran was more than just a service. We hadn't been able to find much information on it. Initially, I'd thought Rachel was working as an escort, but we'd since found that she was managing the escort side.

This didn't surprise me. For all that Rachel was

a stone-cold vindictive bitch, she was a crafty one, and if there was one thing she was good at, it was pulling the wool over people's eyes. I bet he thought she was a dumb blonde, and he was using her. If I was right, she'd have him over the barrel before long and she wouldn't care how she got there. She'd walk over whoever she needed to, to get to the top. Rachel was money hungry, and she craved being the centre of attention. Which is probably why she'd stayed pregnant. She would have loved the attention it afforded her. I just hoped that whatever she did to him didn't blow back on us.

We'd finally found my brother, and the disgust and hurt that filled me at the sight of him probably didn't help the way I was feeling about his son.

Somehow, he'd ended up in Birmingham. He wasn't working, and that's how Skinny had found him because he'd signed on to get benefits. Navy, Bull, Bond, and I'd ridden to Birmingham to the address that Skinny had found.

If I thought the housing estate that Reaper's kids had lived on was bad, I had to rethink that. It was at least two steps up from where my brother was living. Leaving Bull and Bond with the bikes, Navy and I walked up four flights of stairs as there was no way we were getting in the lift. The stairs stank of pee, we saw used needles thrown carelessly on the stairs, and at one part of the staircase there was brown wiped all along the one wall. I wasn't sure if it was dried blood or excrement, but I made sure to stay well away from it.

My skin was crawling by the time we made it to the dirty, dark red door that was on Mike's information.

"Fuck, I'm going to need a shower asap," Navy muttered, voicing what I'd been thinking.

Lifting my hand, I pounded at the door and waited. After a minute, I pounded again. "Jesus Christ, give me a fucking minute," we heard shouted from within. There was some scrabbling and cursing before the door opened.

I took a step back at the smell as Mike filled the door. I couldn't believe that this was my brother. Mike and I'd been built the same. Growing up we'd looked so much alike that most people thought we were twins even though he was two years older than me. Yet here he was, standing in front of me, shrunk to half the size he used to be. His black hair long and unkept, he sported a scruffy unkept beard, bloodshot green eyes the whites yellowing. He wore a greying, dirty vest, and a pair of tracksuit pants that looked like they'd seen better days. I'd clocked the track marks in his arms straight away. That he'd deteriorated so much since I'd last seen him three years ago came as a shock.

"What the fuck do you want?" Mike snarled at me. I grimaced at the smell of his breath, wondering when he'd last brushed his teeth.

"I'm here about your son," I told him.

He started to laugh, manically, "Why? Did that bitch Mel send you after me for money? You can tell her to go fuck herself. She left me so she can suck it up."

I didn't recognise the man in front of me at all. He'd been the one I'd looked up to most of my life. That only changed when I joined up. It was like somehow I'd kept him on an even keel and as soon as I wasn't there to keep him straight, he lost all his moral compass. Then he'd betrayed me by sleeping with my fiancée which was the last straw.

"I'm not here about your and Mel's kids, Mike. I'm here about Kaleb. The boy you had with Rachel."

He shrugged before callously saying, "I'm

guessing she's dumped him on you and that's why you're here. He's not my problem. I told her to put your name on the birth certificate. I already had two kids I didn't want. Why would I want to add a third?"

I had to try one more time, he was my brother and until three years ago we'd been close.

"Mike," I uttered gruffly, but he stopped me holding up a hand, his eyes clear and for just a minute, it was almost like I was looking at the old Mike, "Kev, stop. I've got nothing to offer anyone. The boy is better with you. You'd be a far better father than I could ever be. He's yours. Now fuck off and don't come back."

With that, he shut the door in my face. I stood there for what seemed forever. Finally, Navy clasped my shoulder saying, "Let's go, brother, there's nothing you can do here."

With a nod, I walked away from the door that the man that was my brother in blood had shut in my face. Knowing it would be the last time I'd see him.

I walked away, following a brother that I knew would walk through a hail of bullets for me. I knew this because he'd done it.

Bull and Bond didn't say anything when we got

back to them. They must have seen by the look on my face that the meeting hadn't gone well. We'd mounted our bikes for the trek back home. It was a long, quiet ride.

There was an accident on the motorway, and we'd ended up stuck for a couple of hours before we could get off at the next junction. We'd stopped for something to eat and to stretch our legs before we'd continued. The accident and then stopping had added another three hours on our journey. So, it was past eleven at night before we pulled into the Crow Manor driveway to park.

Parking up, I took my helmet off and ran my hands over my head, then pushing the palms of my hands hard against my eyes, rubbing the tiredness from them.

"You good, brother?" Bull questioned.

Dropping my hands, I look up at his words, seeing the concern on my brothers' faces. I shook off the gloom as best as I could.

"No," I responded honestly. "But I will be."

My brothers were worried for me, I knew this. I needed to pull my head out of my arse and start taking stock of my life. My wallowing and resentment needed to stop; it wasn't me. I also wasn't being fair to Avy, and I'd vowed when I first met her, I'd not make her life harder than it needed to be. And here we were, barely two months into our marriage, and I was letting her down. Not that she'd complained once. That wasn't how my woman worked.

I got a chin lift from Navy, Bond, and Bull, then they called out "Night, brother," as they walked away.

"Night," I responded and got off my bike, stretching my back out.

"He's right you know," Bond said.

I looked up startled, I'd seen him walk away with Navy and Bull.

"I came back," he explained at my start of surprise.

"Who was right?" I quizzed, confused at his words.

"Your brother. I came up to see what was taking so long and happened to catch the last part of your conversation. He was right. Kaleb is better off with you and Avy. You'll be a fantastic father once you get your head out of your arse," he smirked at me.

Tilting my head, I looked at him in surprise,

"How do you know I'll be a good father?"

Bond stared at me for a long moment. I was beginning to think he wasn't going to say anything when he spoke, "I know because my father wasn't a good one. We also know you're beating yourself up worrying about how you're treating your brother's kid and that you should be doing better."

I was shocked that they'd noticed, why I was surprised they'd noticed I wasn't sure. I should have known better. The brotherhood noticed everything. I guess that's what happened when you lived in each other's pockets.

"Yeah, we've noticed," Bond continued. "We've also noticed that while you're struggling with how you feel about him, you've still ensured he's not going without. The day after he was dumped on you, you bought him an entire wardrobe, brother, not knowing if he was staying or not. And not once have you lashed out at him even when he had a meltdown last week. That alone tells me you're already a better dad than some have had. Cut yourself some slack. You're allowed to have doubts and feel angry. Any of us would. Trust me, when you let that little boy in, your life and his are only going to get better."

I was silent for a moment, ruminating on everything Bond had laid out.

"He's a baby, Bond. Of course, I'd make sure he had clothes. And the meltdown last week wasn't his fault. He's had a lot thrown at him the last few weeks. I don't even think you'd call what he had a meltdown as such. He didn't make a sound other than the one scream."

Bond smiled broadly at me, "You're right, brother, he's a baby. He isn't your brother and he sure as fuck isn't that cunt that birthed him. He's his own person. Now, how about maybe you think on if you want that person to turn out to be like you or like them? With you and Avy in his corner, there isn't any way he'd turn out like them."

Inhaling a deep breath, I slowly exhaled, relaxing a little as I breathed out the tension. I understood what he was saying, and he was right. I knew I had to let it go.

"I hear you, Bond, and I'll do better at letting shit go."

"That's all anyone can do. And if you find you need to vent, you come to one of us. If that means you need to pound on one of us, we can handle it or if you just want a beer or a ride, we can do that too. No more of this lone wolf crap. I get as a sniper you're used to being alone, but you also know how to work as part of a team. Your brothers are here to support you, Hawk. And if we can't, then the women are always there. If none of that works, then you go and see someone. Maybe an outside perspective is what you need."

"Okay, brother, I'm hearing you. I'll come looking if shit starts getting too much. I promise. Thank you."

Bond straightened from where he'd been leaning against the garage wall while he schooled me on getting my shit together. I appreciated it. He was one of the quieter brothers. It wasn't often that he offered an opinion. That he had voiced his made me pay attention.

Giving me a salute, he turned to leave. I watched as he wandered off down the path to the cottages.

Dragging my weary arse into the house and up the stairs to our wing. Stopping at the door that had a dim night light shining from it, I pushed it open slightly before entering the room. Walking closer to the single bed we'd put in here a month ago. I'd bolted sides onto it because Avy had been worried he'd fall out. Kaleb was passed out fast asleep, sprawled out on his belly, diapered butt in the air. Pulling the blankets that he'd kicked off back over him, I chuckled quietly at the soft snuffling snore that came out of him. Resting a hand on his back, I looked at him properly for the first time since he'd been left with us and noticed right away that he was looking much healthier, his cheeks were fuller, and he had dimples on his hands. Closing my eyes, I took a deep breath. I'd do better by him. Turning to leave, I stopped when I saw Avy watching from the doorway.

She didn't say anything, just smiled and held out her hand. Taking it, I followed her to our bedroom next door. Still not saying a word, she pushed me into the armchair in the corner of our room, kneeling to take off my socks, my boots long discarded at the kitchen door. Still kneeling, she pulled at my shirt, lifting my arms as I helped her remove it. Avy bit her lip and ran her hands up my legs, tugging at my zipper and button on my pants until they were loose. Looking at me through her lashes, she licked her lower lip. Taking my cock in her hand, she stroked me once then twice before lowering her head and sucking the tip into her mouth.

I let out a growl as she slowly ran her tongue around the head before sucking me deep into her mouth until I hit the back of her throat, letting out a curse as she swallowed. "Fuck," I grunted and tilted my hips, running my fingers through her hair to pull it away from her face so that I could watch my cock disappearing into her lush mouth, lips swollen around me, cheeks flushed. Pulling at the silk dressing gown she had on so that I could get to her skin.

It wasn't like we'd been going without sex; we hadn't, but there was something different about tonight. I didn't know if it was how Avy seemed to need to take care of me tonight or if it was me.

"Fuck, Sweets," I moaned low in my throat as Avy took my balls in her hand and gently tugged on them, then laved her tongue down my length and around my balls, sucking first one and then the other into her mouth. Pre-cum dripped down me and around her fingers. Gasping for breath like I'd run a mile, I put my hand over hers to stop.

"What's wrong," Avy whispered.

"Nothing, I don't want to come in your mouth, I want to come inside you."

With a small smile, she gave me one last lick.

I hissed as her tongue hit my sensitive tip, the neediness of my cock forgotten as Avy rose up and pulled at the belt of her robe letting it slip down her arms and to the floor, she'd been naked underneath, the moon from the open curtains hit her body making it seem as if she glowed. She slid one leg onto the chair and threw the other over my thighs to straddle me, bending to kiss me, her lips wet and a little swollen from having my cock in her mouth. Grabbing my cock, I ran the tip through her wet folds and notched it at her entrance pulling her closer as she sank down, throwing her head back as I filled her up thrusting her tits near to my face close enough that it was easy for me to latch onto a nipple and suck it deep in my mouth. Letting out a guttural groan as her pussy tightened on my cock with each suck. Moving to her other breast, I gave it the same treatment and hissed as she again squeezed my cock with her walls. I wasn't going to be able to last at this rate.

Wetting my thumb, I slipped it between us and pressed it to her clit. My other hand threading through Avy's hair, pulling her head towards me so I could take her mouth in a hard ravishing kiss, our tongues twirling, Avy swivelled her hips seductively as she rode me, her hips swivelling against mine in time with my tongue. Pressing harder on her clit, her hips stuttered to a stop, and she threw back her head and ground down hard, arms tight around my shoulders as I thrust up into her depths, both of us coming hard at the same time.

Breathing raggedly, Avy collapsed against my chest, tucking her head into my shoulder.

"Love you, Avy," I whispered, pressing a kiss to her damp temple. Her mouth moved against my neck, pressing a kiss to my collarbone. Tilting her head back, she looked at me with a small smile gracing her lips.

"Love you too. Missed you today."

"Yeah."

"Yeah." She sat up, cupping my face in her hands as she studied me, her eyes soft and worried. "Navy messaged me. I'm sorry, your visit with your brother didn't go well. I can't say I'm sad that we get to keep Kaleb, though."

Rubbing my nose against hers, I nodded in agreement, "Yeah, we'd best get that paperwork sorted so that we can make him ours, not just mine."

Avy smiled wide at me, happiness made her eyes sparkle a bright blue in the dim light of our bedroom.

"I'll get that sorted tomorrow," she assured me. "Now, how about you carry me to the shower and maybe I'll let you dirty me up again."

Chuckling at her words, I stood with her in my arms and carried her to the bathroom where I made good on dirtying her up again just as she requested.

CHAPTER 14

AVY

Hawk turned a corner after the visit to his brother. I always knew he would. I'd just had to be patient and wait him out. He'd see soon enough how wonderful Kaleb was. Because that baby had stolen everyone's hearts. He was so good natured, and although he was slightly younger than Mila, he seemed older, in that he watched everything around him and seemed to make decisions based on what was going on in the room he was in. It hurt all of us to see him like this because we wondered what hell he'd lived through to make him so wary.

He was also extremely protective over me as Rogue had found out when we'd been messing around in the kitchen and he'd grabbed hold of me and tickled me, making me shriek with laughter, something we'd done countless times and not thought anything of. Everyone had been laughing except for one small tornado who'd attacked Rogue, punching at his leg with his little fists, shouting NO loudly. Kaleb had a surprisingly deep voice for someone so small. When Rogue had realised that we were upsetting him, he'd stopped immediately, and I'd stooped and picked Kaleb up and plopped him on my hip. His little face had been fierce and the scowl he'd worn was something to see. I didn't know if I should laugh or not because he was just too cute for words.

"It's okay, Kaleb. Uncle Rogue was just playing," I assured him, pressing a kiss to his head.

He'd ignored me and held up a finger to Rogue, "No hurt. Mine."

My heart had just about exploded from my chest with happiness, and I couldn't help the smile that had bloomed across my face.

Rogue had nodded seriously, and shook Kaleb's hand, "Okay, little man, I get it. Nobody hurts Avy."

Seeming to accept what Rogue had said, Kaleb had given him a blinding smile before hugging my neck and then squirming until I put him down. He toddled back off to play with Mila on the far side of the kitchen, but not before stopping to scowl over his shoulder once more to make sure that Rogue was behaving. Julia had let out a giggle, and I'd sniggered at the look on Rogue's face.

Reaper had grinned at Rogue, "I guess that told you, brother," he snorted out a laugh, "bested by a two-year-old."

Rogue shook his head with a chuckle, "He's fierce, he'll be a force in about twenty years."

While the rest of the brotherhood was teasing Rogue, I was watching Hawk, who hadn't taken his eyes off Kaleb. They'd softened, and he had a small proud smile curling the corner of his lips. Then he ran his hand gently over his nephew's head as he walked past. It was just fleeting, but Kaleb noticed and looked up. Two pairs of green eyes stared at each other, neither giving an inch. Suddenly Hawk smiled a full smile at Kaleb, ruffled his hair a little and continued out the kitchen to wherever he'd been going.

My eyes caught my mum's, and she smiled at me. Slowly but surely over the next few weeks, the two of them became more familiar with each other. Kaleb didn't tense every time Hawk walked into a room and Hawk found a way to show him the smallest bit of affection whenever he could.

It seemed they'd bonded over their need to keep

me safe and looked after.

Kaleb had been with us for nearly two months when the final breakthrough happened.

A storm had been forecast with gale force winds and rain. It was meant to get very bad during the night but should blow over by the next day.

I'd woken up to the wind howling, and the rain was lashing at the windows, lightening flashing through the room. I realised I was alone in bed and wondered where Hawk had gone, deciding I'd better check on Kaleb. I hoped that the storm hadn't woken him up. Getting up, I pulled on my dressing gown, shoved my cold feet into slippers and left the room. I stopped just outside Kaleb's room when I heard Hawk's voice.

"Hey, little man, you doing okay?" he whispered softly. I heard a rustle then a soft whimper as another flash of lightening lit up the room.

"Hey, hey, shhh, it's okay, nothing to be scared of, I won't let anything hurt you," Hawk continued to talk softly to Kaleb, "come on, little man, let's go. You can sleep with me and Avy tonight."

My heart just about melted into a puddle at Hawk's tone of voice. Not wanting to make a big deal out of it and be caught listening to his moment with Kaleb, I hurried back to our room, stripped off my dressing gown and dove into bed, waiting for them to come and join me. I'd just got myself comfortable when Hawk walked in with Kaleb in his arms. I'm sure my ovaries exploded.

Was there anything hotter than a man with a baby, especially when that baby was the spitting image of them?

I smiled when they got to the side of the bed, asking softly, "Everything okay?"

"Of course. We're going to have a sleepover tonight," Hawk said, lowering Kaleb to the bed who didn't waste any time snuggling into me.

"Is that right?"

"Yep," Hawk answered getting into bed and pulling the covers up over us. Turning on his side, he laid an arm across Kaleb and cupped my hip. Kaleb had already fallen asleep, knowing he was safe between us.

God, I loved this man.

"Love you, Hawk. I'm proud to have you as my man," I whispered in the darkness.

His breath hitched, and the hand that had been under his head reached across the pillows for mine. He twined his fingers through mine. His eyes gleamed in the darkness as they sought mine.

"I'm sorry it took me so long to get here, Sweets."

"No apology needed, Hawk. I knew you'd get here, you just needed time. He'll have a good life with us," I promised.

"Yeah, he will," Hawk said softly, pressing a kiss to Kaleb's hair.

It didn't take long for us to fall asleep listening to the storm that ran wild outside.

I woke just after seven to Kaleb's foot in my face, pushing up against my nose, making it hard to breathe. Gently, I moved it back to the bed. Sitting up, I smiled and reached for my phone to take a picture of my two sleeping boys. Kaleb had moved away from me during the night and was sprawled across Hawk's chest. Hawk had his hand under his little butt, holding Kaleb to his chest. It was the perfect photo, so I took it and promptly shared it with the rest of the family. Knowing they'd understand what it meant for us.

Getting up, I got ready for the day, knowing that I wasn't going to enjoy what I had to do today. I'd be finalising Kaleb's registration at the nursery that Mila went to. I'd taken time off when Kaleb came into our lives to settle him with us. I needed to get back to work, so he'd be starting this week at the same nursery where Mila went and I wasn't looking forward to not spending all day, every day with him.

Hawk and I had decided that we'd only put him in three half days for now and if it all went okay, we'd up his days to five half days.

Now that Kaleb had come into our lives, Mum had decided to semi-retire so she could spend more time with him and Ellie. As had Aunt Maggie. Between the two of them, they said they'd cover the children in the afternoons. We'd see how it all went. I didn't want them to be tired out.

Leaving Hawk and Kaleb to sleep, I got dressed and headed out to the nursery and then on to the pub for a bit to check in with everyone.

I'd asked Hawk to drop Kaleb off at the pub on his way to work today but left him a note anyway.

Good morning,

You both looked comfortable, so I didn't want to wake you up. I'll be at the pub at about tenish. Drop

Kaleb off with me there.

Love you both.

Xoxoxo

CHAPTER 15

HAWK

It had been a few weeks since the night of the storm and Avy, Kaleb, and I'd settled into a routine.

I looked up from where I was sitting on the couch in the reception when the bell over the door in the tattoo shop dinged. I'd been sitting here drawing while I waited for my next client. I smiled when Avy and Kaleb walked in. He squirmed in her arms as soon as he saw me, and she laughed, putting him down.

He ran over and climbed up on the couch, plonking himself down next to me and looking at what I'd been drawing.

"Hi, Sweets, what are you two doing here?" I asked as I tilted my head to receive the kiss that I knew she'd give me.

Avy smiled happily at me, doing exactly what I expected. Pressing her lips to mine, I threaded my hand into her hair at the back of head and held her to me as I deepened the kiss.

"Mmh," Avy murmured when I let her up for air, "I missed you and knew you'd be working late, so I thought Kaleb and I'd join you for an early supper." Avy explained, holding up the bag she held in her right hand.

"You must have read my mind; I was just about to go to the café for something but got sidetracked by this design."

Looking down at the top of Kaleb's head as he studied my designs, I wondered what he was thinking. It was a nautical scene and would be going on Navy; it had an octopus pulling an old-style ship into the depths of the sea with a nautical compass imprinted in the head of the octopus. It was a beautiful piece, and I was looking forward to adding it to him. I already knew he wanted it on his shoulder.

Nudging Kaleb's shoulder, he looked up at me, "Do you like it?" I asked gesturing to the page.

He nodded his head but didn't say anything else. We'd got used to his quietness. He spoke when needed, but otherwise, he was still a quiet child.

It was hard to believe he'd been with us for four months now. I'd known that Rachel wouldn't be back for him after the month like she'd said she would.

Avy had insisted we hold a birthday party for him last week. It had been his third birthday. The look on his face when Avy had brought out his cake – his eyes were so big they took up most of his face and the smile of delight that he'd had when she put it in front of him. It made Avy's day. Cally had been taking photos, and she'd caught him at just the right moment. Avy had the picture blown up, and I'd hung it in our hallway along with our wedding pictures.

I nudged him again, and when he looked at me, I asked, "You hungry?" He nodded, closing my sketch pad gently. Taking it from him, I put it on the table and then grabbed him, and blew on his belly, making him squeal with laughter, before hanging him upside down by his feet. His laughter gurgled out of him in a deep chuckle. Avy beamed a wide smile at us before turning to walk to the kitchen.

"More," Kaleb shouted. I laughed and pretended to eat his belly, blowing loud raspberries on it. He was still laughing when I pulled him up and turned him the right way up, settling him on my hip.

Wrapping his arms around my neck, he hugged me tight. "Daddy, funny."

I jerked to a stop as Avy's wide eyes hit mine. It was the first time he'd called me Dad. He'd started calling Avy, Mummy about six weeks ago, but he'd not called me anything. I cleared the sudden lump from my throat and smiled wide at him.

"I'm funny, huh," I teased, tickling him. Nodding his head, he squirmed against me, laughing his little head off. When he stopped laughing, I hugged him tight and kissed his head before depositing him in the chair next to Avy.

"This looks good, Sweets," I said, sitting down. Avy had brought thick roast beef and horseradish sandwiches for us, crisps, fruit and drinks. It looked like Kaleb's was cheese. Helping her, I dished up for Kaleb.

It was good to spend time with just the three of us. We got caught up on her day, Kaleb's morning at nursery and what was happening with the pub.

We hadn't had time to connect as a family, just the three of us for a while. The reason for that was that it had been crazy over at the main house, as all the babies had been born in the last few months.

Reaper and Abby, Onyx and Rea had each had a

boy, and Draco and Molly had a girl. While it had admittedly been crazy and chaotic, it was a good crazy.

CHAPTER 16

AVY

Another early morning found me rushing out of the house with Kaleb and Mila in tow. My quiet supper with Hawk and Kaleb last night a distant memory.

It was my turn to drop them off at nursery, as Rea was busy with the new baby. Getting them buckled into the car seats was a feat. But once I had them in the car and I was ready to go, the rest of the ride into the village was fun. We sang nursery rhymes most of the way. The two of them were cute as they tried to get their tongue around some of the wordier sounds.

The nursery car park was busy as usual. Carrying Kaleb, I held onto Mila's hand, taking them to be signed in. Kaleb and Mila's usual nursery nurse wasn't there to meet us; instead, there was what I assumed was a temp. She was a little brusque when I signed the two of them in not like the usual nursery nurse Sally, who was both friendly and funny. I didn't have a good feeling, and almost didn't leave them, but instead decided to talk to the manager first to find out who she was. Hugging and kissing them both goodbye, neither seemed concerned about not seeing a familiar face.

In the background, I caught sight of one of the other familiar staff members and she'd given me a friendly wave and welcomed both the children and helped them hang up their bags and sit on the mat in their room. The familiarity made me feel better.

I stopped at the manager's office, anyway. Her door was usually open for parents at this time of the morning. Carol's head lifted up at my knock on the door frame, and she smiled when she saw me.

"Avy," Carol greeted. "What can I do for you?"

"Morning Carol, I just wanted to check who the new member of staff was. I was wondering where Sally was today."

Carol made a face, "Sally had a car accident on her way home last night. She's in the hospital but should be released soon."

I felt bad for Sally on hearing the news, "Oh poor Sally, I hope she's okay."

Carol nodded, "She'll be fine. She broke her leg

and has a concussion so won't be back at work for a while. We've had to get a temp in."

"Yeah, that's why I'm here. I wanted to check that she's up to speed on who can pick up Kaleb and Mila."

Carol smiled, "Don't worry, we've let her know, and she's been updated on all the safety protocols. You don't have to worry about the children, Avy, they'll be safe. My word."

Feeling a little better, I thanked her and left, hurrying to the pub to get on with ordering and organising a band for this weekend. I'd been at work about two hours when my phone rang. Seeing it was the nursery number, I answered it, wondering if one of the children needed picking up early.

Answering the phone, I could hear straight away that there was something wrong. My heart sank at her words. Carol started speaking in a panicked tone as soon as I answered the phone, "Avy, oh my god. I'm so sorry. Kaleb's missing."

"What?!" I shouted, standing up rapidly, my chair hitting the wall behind me.

"No, no, no!!" I shouted, agony tearing through me at her words. "You said just this morning you had procedures in place."

I started to shake, wondering how this was happening. We'd put procedures in place to stop just such a thing from occurring in case Rachel turned up and tried to take him. One of my staff members put their head around the corner at my shout. I didn't look up to see who it was. I just shouted at them to get Hawk. Grabbing my car keys, I ignored Carol, who was sobbing and kept apologising that she was sorry. That they were all sorry.

"Sorry doesn't help, Carol. My son is fucking missing, you stupid bitch. He's missing on your watch. My husband and I will be there soon."

I ran out of the pub to my car; I was shaking so bad that I knew I shouldn't be driving. Hearing Hawk shout my name, I stopped and turned; I crumpled as soon as I saw him.

He caught me just before I hit the ground. I was sobbing uncontrollably. "He's gone, Hawk, someone took him from nursery. Someone took our son," I sobbed against his chest. I felt like my heart had been wrenched out of my body.

Kaleb had only been mine for a few short months. I may not have birthed him, but he was mine.

Hawk tensed at my words, "What? Baby, you

need to calm down and tell me exactly what's happened to Kaleb."

Stepping out of his arms, I took a deep breath, and then another, trying to control my breathing. By now, all the MC that had been in town was on the street with us. Tears welled in my eyes again, but I held them back. I'd had my breakdown and crying wasn't going to find him.

"Kaleb is missing from the nursery. Somebody has taken him, that's all I know. We need to get there and get there now," I cried out brokenly.

Various cries and curses echoed around us at my news. Hawk's face paled, and he lifted a shaky hand to his mouth, before closing his eyes. When he opened them again, they were stone cold and focused.

Turning around, he pointed at Skinny, snapping out an order, "Get into the nursery's security system and find out who took my son." Skinny saluted and ran down the street towards his bike taking off at speed towards the manor where he had his set up.

"Somebody call Reaper and let him know," Hawk continued. "And then I need one of you to drive Avy and me to the nursery, I'm not steady enough to do it."

"I'll take you," Rogue offered. "We'll need to pick Mila up, anyway."

"Oh my god, Mila," I whispered, feeling guilty. "How could I forget her? I hope she's okay."

"We'll meet you back at Crow Manor," Navy advised as he and Bond jogged back towards the gym.

"I'll see everyone is updated," Carly said, reaching out to hug me blinking back tears. "Please keep us informed of any news. We'll start closing down the businesses so we can help look."

Nodding that I would do that, I took the hand Hawk held out to me and jogged to the car with him. Getting in just as my phone rang. Seeing it was Reaper, I put it on speaker, answering tearfully, "Kane, someone took him."

"I know, Avs, I'm sorry, sis. Can you fill us in?"

"I don't know anything else, we're just on our way to the nursery. Rogue is driving us, and we'll get Mila. Hawk has asked Skinny to check the security footage so that we can see who it was. It can't have been Rachel because they had a photo of her and knew not to let him go with her. I'll give you a call back as soon as I can, we're just pulling into the nursery car park. Greg is here so

I'll see what he has to say," I snivelled, wiping at my nose and eyes, as we pulled into the parking lot and stopped next to the patrol car.

The car hadn't even come to a stop and Hawk was out and stalking towards Carol and Greg. Saying goodbye, I ended the call and got out. Rogue put his arm around my shoulders.

Hawk was furious. He was pointing a finger in Carol's face when we got to them. If ever anybody thought he didn't love Kaleb, they'd know they were wrong.

"You had better hope we find my son and that not a hair on his head has been hurt," Hawk raged at her. "Now go and get my niece, so that we can get her home to her parents, where she'll be safe."

Carol winced at his words but didn't say anything, just turned and walked back into the nursery to do as he bid.

Hawk turned to Greg, "What do you know?"

"Not much, other than they had some temp staff and one of them is missing. I'm assuming she's the one that took Kaleb. They've given us access to the security footage, and we'll check it again, but my guess is that the person who took him was the temp woman."

"Come with me," Greg said, lowering his voice as he took Hawk's arm, walking him further away from his colleagues. Rogue and I followed on behind them.

"I've sent Skinny the video to save time. I've also sent him the woman's name and all the information I could find on her. I hope that's enough for him to work with. It will be quicker for you guys to look than it will for me to go via our channels."

"Thank you, Greg," I whispered.

"I hope you find him, Avy. I don't have to tell you that time is of the essence in these cases. You know that already. To keep the rest of my colleagues from you, I've volunteered myself and Rod to come and get a statement. Rod is the type to turn a blind eye, especially in cases such as these. Once you get Mila, head home and we'll follow."

Hawk nodded. Reaching for me, he wrapped an arm around me and pulled me tight to his side. I could feel the tears welling again. Kaleb had been through so much in his short life, it wasn't fair that he'd have to go through more.

Just then Carol came out with Mila, Rogue left us to go and get her. Saying goodbye to Gary, Hawk and I walked back to our car. Carol tried to say something as we walked past her, but I ignored her. I couldn't look at her. I was itching to hit something and if she said the wrong thing, it would be her.

We needed to get home and see what had been found. My heart hurt, I just hoped that wherever Kaleb was he was okay.

CHAPTER 17

HAWK

Breathing deeply, I watched as the sun slowly rose. There was a foggy mist hanging over the trees this morning, but it looked like it was going to be a beautiful day. I just wished that we could enjoy it.

It had been eighteen hours since Kaleb had gone missing from his supposedly secure nursery. It was all over the news, causing a shit storm as we were harassed by reporters. I'd had to watch as Avy slowly fell apart at each passing hour. We'd done an interview on the front lawn, there had been a police liaison officer and our lawyer with us. We'd appealed but had not had any further news.

To further murky the waters, the woman who had abducted him had been found this morning in an alley in London with her throat slit.

Skinny was scouring the internet as well as the dark web to try and find something. Anything on her. But she'd seemed to be clean other than owing a shit tonne of money for a gambling debt. Skinny was pulling strings to find out who it was she owed.

The inaction was killing me, but I knew it was pointless to start rushing out without having any direction of where to look. I'd tried to reach out to Rachel but had got an out-of-order tone on her mobile. We'd driven to her last known address, but she hadn't been there and by the amount of mail in her post-box in the lobby of where her flat was, it looked like she hadn't been home for a while. We'd still gone up to check her flat. Bond had managed to pick the lock. The place was dusty and had the musty air smell of having been locked up for a while. Rachel must still be abroad with her sugar daddy/boss.

While we'd been in the city, we'd also checked out his nightclub again. It was Bond that came through. He'd recognised one of the bouncers on the door as being from his old neighbourhood and had gone to speak to him while we waited with the bikes. We'd watched as they'd had a long conversation, then Bond had laughed, slapped the guy on the shoulder, pulled him in for a hug while shaking his hand. I couldn't be sure, but it looked like Bond slipped him some cash.

Navy caught my eye; we waited until Bond came back. He started speaking as soon as he was back with us, "Cole says they came back day before yesterday. But he hasn't seen either one of them since then. He doesn't know where they went after they left here."

'Well, at least it was something' I thought.

"Thanks, Bond, it's better than nothing. How much did that cost you?" I asked.

Scowling at me, he grunted, "It's irrelevant, Kaleb is family. I'd pay anything for information to find out where he is."

Clearing my throat to get rid of the lump that had formed at his words, "Thank you, brother," I told him.

Bond nodded at me, not replying, just put his helmet on and got on his bike, ready to get back home. Hopefully, with this new information, Skinny would be able to find something out.

That had been last night. Skinny had been locked in his room since then, only leaving to use the bathroom or get something to drink. We had to get a break. I just hoped to Christ it was soon because I felt like I was about to come out of my skin.

We'd finally managed to persuade Avy to lie down to rest, although I'd found out after the fact that Rea had slipped something into a cup of tea she'd given her. But at least she'd get a few hours of respite. There was no way I could sleep. I missed my little man like I was missing a limb. He'd slowly worked his way deep into my heart. I'm not sure what I would do if we didn't find him soon.

Just then, from inside the clubhouse, Skinny gave a loud curse and shouted out my name in a panicked tone, "Hawk!"

Jumping to my feet, I rushed back into the clubhouse straight into Skinny's room. Not stopping until I skidded to a halt and took a good look at my brother; he was pale and had bloodshot red eyes from the hours he'd been stuck at his screens. Empty coffee cups and energy drinks littered his desks.

"Did you find something?!" I barked as soon as I was in the room.

The rest of the brotherhood had followed me in as I ran past where they had all been dozing or sleeping in the chairs in the main room.

"Sort of. It wasn't me that found it. I was sent it and it's not good, brother."

Walking around his desk to have a look at his screen and my stomach sank.

"Fuck," I whispered hoarsely, "we can't let Avy know."

There on the screen, along with another toddler locked in a cage, was my son. His face swollen from crying, dirty tracks showing on his face from his tears. The other toddler looked like a little girl, they were holding tight onto each other, asleep for now which was a small mercy. What had scared me and had my stomach sinking was the clock in the right-hand corner that was counting down from thirty hours. I knew what that meant. Thirty hours and he'd be up for sale. We'd never find him then. I didn't want to think about what would happen to him once he was sold.

Curses echoed around the room as each of my brothers saw what was on the screen.

"How did you find this?" I asked Skinny.

"That's the thing, I didn't," Skinny replied, looking a little freaked out about the whole thing.

"What do you mean you didn't find it?" Reaper barked.

"It was sent to me with a message stating it was

from a friend. They also said to give them twelve hours and they would have him back with us. It was signed: **Friend of the Hawk**."

Running a shaky hand down my face, my hand rasped against my beard, and I rubbed at my eyes. I had no clue who this person was that said they were my friend but if I ever found out, I'd be owing them until the end of time.

"Can you reply back and ask if they need help with the extraction?" Reaper ordered.

We waited as Skinny typed out the message. A reply wasn't long in coming back.

'No help needed. You'd slow us down. The boy will be safe. Mother is dead. Tried to save boy from sale. Her boss will be punished for selling him.'

"Fuck," Draco said. "Who the fuck are these people?"

"What about the little girl?" I said to Skinny. "Find out about her."

Skinny again typed and we waited.

'Good family. Will drop back at house. I know hard. Patience, friends.'

The chat box went dead, but the video stayed up, showing the bids in the corner. I felt sick.

What was wrong with people that they would hurt children like this? I'd seen horrific things during my time in the military, but the things that happened to children always hit different. They were innocents drawn into adult games that they had no chance of winning. It made me sick.

The room was silent. Whoever had sent us a link to the video had left it on so we could watch the children. I didn't know if this was worse than the not knowing.

Seeing him so close but unable to hold him, it was killing me. I'd had to walk away when one of his captors had come in with water, had pretended to give it to them, then take it away teasing them.

Kaleb had only fallen for it twice, then he'd done his usual stare and ignored the twastard, but the little girl with him had cried and cried. I'd never been so proud of my son as I was when he put his arm around her and pulled her close, holding her tight. His lips moved so he must have said something to her and I wished I knew what. The pillick teasing them dropped the bottle of water through the bars of the cage once he stopped getting a reaction. We cursed as we watched Kaleb struggle to open the bottle, his little hand not quite strong enough.

Not being able to watch anymore, I walked away before I hit something. How fucking cruel could you be? I was walking up and down the road outside the clubhouse, glad that Avy hadn't seen it.

Rubbing at the stinging in my eyes, my breaths coming thick and fast. Stopping my pacing, I stood in the middle of the road looking up at the blue sky, it was such a peaceful morning. A perfect spring day. Taking a deep breath of fresh air and then another one until my breathing evened out and the urge to cry and scream was contained. I counted blessings.

One - for now he was fine, we could see him. We'd handle dehydration and hunger when he was home.

Two – I had no idea who my friend was, but I was thankful for them.

Three - if whoever my friend was, was telling the truth, then Kaleb would be home by tonight.

Four - Skinny was still looking for him even if my friend had said not to. I had to have faith. Not many people were lucky enough to have the connections that we did or the support that we had.

With one last deep breath, I turned and walked back to the clubhouse, stopping when Navy walked out the doors. He held up a hand, "He's fine. Not sure who your friends are, but once the fucker left, the cameras went dark for a while as if there was a glitch and when it came back Kaleb and the little girl were drinking from the bottle of water. My guess whoever the rescuers are, they are special forces or ex-special forces and are already situated waiting for the right moment. It's what I would do."

"Okay," I acknowledge, huffing out a breath. "I wonder who they are?"

Navy shrugged, "I guess we'll find out tonight. Praying their op goes according to plan and that they can extract the kids without any issues."

Striding back to the clubhouse, I pull open the heavy wooden door and walk in.

Reaper came out of Skinny's room. The rest of the brothers had left after we'd got the message about not interfering and were out running the businesses and dodging reporters. After the message had come through asking us not to interfere, Reaper had asked me what I wanted to do.

It seemed pointless for us all sitting around

doing nothing, so I'd told them to go back to work but to put up a sign in the tattoo shop saying it was closed until further notice due to a family emergency.

"How you doing, Hawk?"

"Struggling, Pres. I know when he first arrived, I didn't treat him like I should, but then he crept into my heart and under my skin. He's mine and Avy's son and … fuuuuck," I breathed out through my nose, closing my eyes as tears welled up again.

Lifting my eyes, anguish deepening my voice, "I'm worried that I'm trusting whoever this is with my son's life and that they aren't being honest. What if it's a mistake trusting them? But we have nothing. Skinny is still searching, and he's not found anything new. What the fuck do I do if it all goes pear shaped? How do I tell Avy that I put trust in complete strangers on a feeling in my gut?"

Reaper grabbed me by the back of my neck, pulling me to him, pressing his forehead against mine. "Nothing I say is going to make any of this easier, Hawk. But I have faith that whoever this is will keep their word. Sometimes you just have to have faith."

With one last clap on my back, Reaper let me go. I left him and Navy talking quietly in the common room. I entered Skinny's room, catching him rubbing his eyes tiredly.

Clasping his shoulder, I told him, "Go shower, brother. Catch some kip. There's not much else you can do for now."

"You're right," he agreed. "I did find out why Kaleb was taken though, and I don't think you're going to be happy, although probably not surprised."

"Rachel," I muttered. "Fuck!!!"

"Yeah, but not for the reasons that you think. I don't think she knew they were going to take him."

"Explain," I growled with frustration, not at Skinny but at Rachel.

"I would, but I think it's best you read her email. You know I've been monitoring all our emails in case we got a ransom demand. Well, I was going through them to check, make sure I didn't miss anything. Found it in your spam folder. Explains a lot."

He clicked on a tab on his desktop, opening my email, before getting up from his chair, "There it is. I'll go shower, but I'll be back. I'll catch some sleep on the couch. That way I'm here if you need me."

Nodding my head in agreement, I sat down in his chair, checking on Kaleb and the little girl, before turning my attention to the email. Hardly noticing when Skinny left the room.

Kevin,

Jesus, I hope this gets through to you. They took my phone and changed the password on my computer, but the idiots wrote it down in front of me and I memorised it.

Fuck Kev, I've seriously fucked up this time. I hope this gets to you in time. I don't think I'll be getting out of this alive.

You need to keep Kaleb safe. My boss has threatened him to get back at me for stealing from him.

You probably know by now what I do, who I work for, and all that. I did my research on your club so I know you have someone that can find out stuff about me, and I imagine he's found out everything that he can.

I love my job and it makes me a lot of money, but you know me, I always want more. I started skimming off my boss just a little here and a little there. I've been doing it for two years. At first it was just a thrill thing to see if I could do it and it escalated from there until it was every three months, then every two, until I was skimming weekly. I've banked over three million pounds in the last two years.

I probably would have carried on, but he took me away again last week and while we were away, he brought in an accountant to go through everything. He didn't say anything until the last day when we were coming back. Then he showed me everything. I've given it all back but his last words to me before he left me in my office with the door locked was that my flesh and blood was going to pay for the error in my judgment and that he already had a buyer set up for a baby boy.

If I can get more information to you, I will. I've added an address of where I think they'll take him, but I'm not sure how long they'll be there. If you don't get this in time and he's there I'll try my best to get him out. I have a way out of my office that they don't know about.

For what it's worth, I'm sorry. I did love you, but you know me, I'm never happy unless I'm the centre of attention. I'm sorry I cheated on you and I'm sorry I wrecked Mike's life. It's probably best it ends this way. Kaleb will have a better life with you and your wife. I'm a shitty mum and I'd ruin him.

Look after him and maybe tell him of some of our good times when I wasn't such a stupid cow.

Rachel

x

I didn't know what to think after reading that letter, at least now I knew why they targeted Kaleb. She sure fucked up this time, and a little boy was paying for it. I brought up the address she sent me and saw that it was on the docks in London.

A chat box popped up on the corner of the screen that showed a now sleeping Kaleb.

Right address. Don't come. He's safe for now. Stick with plan!

Fuck! Somehow, they were in our system.

Trust Hawk. Right Path.

I smiled wide, when those exact word appeared I knew who it was. I breathed a sigh of relief for the first time since yesterday morning.

"YES!!" I shouted out.

Reaper and Navy appeared in the doorway.

"What's happened, is he free?" Reaper

questioned impatiently.

"No. Shit, sorry. I just figured out who is messaging us."

Now they were interested. "Well, spit it out," huffed Reaper, impatience clear on his face.

"Do you know the four bikers that come to me whenever the one brother wants a new tattoo? They look like Vikings, never wear helmets."

Both Reaper and Navy nodded.

"It's them, they left another message."

Both Reaper and Navy relaxed their stance. "Thank fuck," Reaper said softly. "At least we know they're friendlies."

There was a loud bang from the common room, and we jumped, then winced when Avy shouted angrily, "Who the fuck gave Rea permission to drug me? And what's happening on finding my son?"

To be fair, I don't think anyone told Rea to sedate Avy, she did it because she knew Avy needed a break.

I stood up from the chair, Navy taking my place to watch the screen and walked out to the common area to find my very angry wife, hands on hips, eyes flashing as she paced up and down.

"Sweets," I said gently.

"Fuck you and your sweets, Hawk. You allowed them to drug me while our son is missing and now I don't know what's happening," Avy ground out as she stopped in front of me.

Reaching out, I grabbed her and pulled her to me, needing to feel her in my arms even if she was angry with me.

"We know where he is," I whispered against her temple. Jerking back, Avy looked at me, "Well, why are you all standing here twiddling your balls? Why isn't he home?"

I'd rather have this Avy – an angry Avy was far better than a sad Avy.

Twining my fingers with hers, I pulled her to Skinny's office, explaining, "I think it's better if I show you first and then explain. Ignore the timer in the corner and people bidding on our son. It's not going to happen."

Navy got up off the chair so that Avy could sit down, tears instantly welled in her eyes until they were overflowing down her cheeks, "Oh, baby boy, those fucking bastards," she whispered, pressing the tips of her fingers to the screen as if she could touch him.

Another chat box opened up with a message

before disappearing just as quickly.

Tell wife. Safe. Bring home. Soon.

Well, that answered my internal question on how they seemed to know what we were saying and doing. Somehow, they were in our systems and could hear and see us.

Avy looked at me with wide eyes, "I think you had better bring me up to speed."

Pulling her up off the chair, I sat down and pulled her back down to sit on my lap so that we could watch Kaleb as he slept. I'm guessing the water they'd been given had been drugged. I filled her in on what had been happening.

Throughout the day we'd all taken turns watching the monitor, but Avy and I had been at the computer for the last hour. I had a feeling it would be happening soon.

It was midnight when another message popped up.

Go Time. Video Off. Home Soon.

Avy let out a pained cry as the screen went blank, Kaleb's image gone. Before turning into me and crying her eyes out. I held on tight, hoping and praying that my faith in the four strange bikers wasn't unfounded.

CHAPTER 18

AVY

Waking up, my head foggy, my mouth tasting like something had set up home and died in it and my bladder so full it actually hurt. My first thought was that we must have partied hard last night and then the day came back to me with a rush, and I doubled over. The pain I felt when I remembered that Kaleb was missing was a physical pain.

Taking deep breaths until I calmed down, I stood up from my bed and stomped angrily to the bathroom to do my thing. Once I was done, I stormed downstairs to find out which motherfucker drugged me. Nobody was home, so I grabbed some fruit on my way out and stormed over to the clubhouse, slamming open the door with a bang. There was nobody in the main common room. Reaper and Hawk came out of Skinny's office at my angry shout.

I almost broke when Hawk took me in his arms, then I did break when I saw Kaleb's sweet face on the screen with that bloody timer counting down and the astronomical amount of money being bid getting higher and higher. My stomach hurt thinking about the sick fucks that were bidding on two babies. Hawk filled me in on what was happening, and we spent the rest of the day watching Kaleb and the little girl with him sleep for most of it. Hawk thought they'd been drugged because they'd been asleep for a long time.

When we'd got the message that the screen was being switched off, I cried, hoping against hope that he'd be home soon.

Two o'clock found Hawk and me pacing up and down the common room. Everyone was with us except for the new mothers and babies, who we'd sent home.

Rea had told me to wake her up when Kaleb got home so that she could check him out.

Three o'clock found us drinking cup after cup of coffee, as we still hadn't heard any news. By the time four o'clock rolled round, all of us were on our feet and Skinny was trying to find any news on what was happening. All we'd been able to find so far was that a warehouse on the docks had blown up and was on fire, the fire had been controlled before it could spread. All available fire engines had been called out to the blaze.

Four-thirty found Hawk pulling on his hair nervously. I knew him. He was worried that he'd put his trust in the wrong people, but I didn't think so.

It was close to five am when we heard the sound of the bikes, and I started running towards the main gate. Reaper had already opened it when four bikes rolled in with the giants that had been waiting for Hawk outside his shop all those months ago.

I skidded to a stop and waited for them to switch their bikes off, Hawk next to me as we scanned them, wondering if there was a vehicle following them because I couldn't see Kaleb anywhere.

Lifting shaking hands to my mouth, I beseechingly whispered, "Where is he?"

The biker that had spoken to Hawk, lifted a hand to the zip on his coat and started to pull it down. There, safe and warm against his chest, nestled Kaleb. He lifted his head and as soon as he saw us, started squirming, saying repeatedly, "Mummy, Mummy."

That was it. I couldn't wait any longer. I rushed over and took him from Silas, hugging and kissing him all over his face. Hawk's arms wrapped around us, his shoulders shaking, then he took Kaleb from me and hugged him, pressing a kiss to his head, whispering brokenly, "I missed you, little man."

My heart was full, we had him back. Without thinking, I threw my arms around Silas, ignoring the way he stiffened at my touch. The man was going to get a thank you hug, whether he liked it or not.

"Thank you. Thank you for bringing him home."

Awkwardly, he patted my back, and in a deep voice that seemed a little rusty, like it didn't get used much, he replied, "You're welcome."

Hawk brought Kaleb back to me. I knew the rest of the family would want to see him, but for now, they were holding back. Reaper was talking to one of the bikers, probably introducing himself. I laughed and it may have had a slight touch of hysteria to it when Kaleb said in a serious tone, "Daddy, I no like those peoples."

"I know, buddy, I no like them either," Hawk told him, handing him back to me where he snuggled his little head right into me.

"Love you, baby boy."

"Luff you, Mummy."

With those words, my soul was complete. I went around and thanked the rest of the bikers; I can't lie, they freaked me out a little bit because they were scary as fuck. But I would be forever grateful for them. We invited them to stay and have something to eat, but they assured us they had to get going. Not twenty minutes after they pulled in, they were gone again.

It made me wonder where they lived. At least we now had their names: Cahir was the leader or what we would consider the president if we were thinking in terms of motorcycle clubs. Silas was his second in command or VP, Cai was his advisor although the man didn't talk so I wasn't sure who he advised but I guess he had his ways and Ramzi was the techy one and it had been him we'd been speaking to on the chats.

Once everyone had welcomed Kaleb home and Rea had checked him over, Hawk and I bathed him and, with no discussion, we took him to bed with us. Neither of us would be able to sleep without him being within touching distance.

It would be a long time before I would be comfortable leaving him anywhere.

With that thought in mind, I drifted off to sleep, Hawk behind me and Kaleb in front, both Hawk's and my arms holding him to us.

It was late afternoon when we woke up and I knew it was going to take a couple of days until we were back in a routine.

I was buzzing with plans already forming. I wasn't going to be putting Kaleb back in a nursery that I didn't think was safe.

Hawk kissed us both goodbye, as he had to get back to the shop. My managers had told me they were fine and that they would manage but would call me if there was an emergency. We'd notified Greg that Kaleb had been found and with Reaper's help, he had put out a simple statement that Kaleb's mother had taken him but had felt guilty and he'd been dropped off at our gates this morning and that no, the police didn't know where she was, but they were looking for her. The simpler, the better we thought.

I put a call out to all the women in our club; it wasn't long and we were all congregated around the kitchen table to brain storm my idea of opening our own nursery on our property. We'd run background checks on the staff, and it would be secure within our fences. With our growing families it would be needed, and I pointed out that if I was going to be lining someone's pocket by paying for childcare, I would rather it be ours.

Julia immediately put a call in to her brother and he said he'd be out the next morning to have a look, organise planning and get a quote to us.

Kaleb started to have nightmares the night after he arrived back home, and it took weeks of care, love, and attention, but they eventually dwindled back until he was sleeping through the night.

He was a mummy's boy through and through, but when Hawk was around then he was a daddy's boy. Made me wonder what this next one was going to be like.

About three months after Kaleb had been kidnapped, it suddenly hit me that I hadn't had a period for a while. Not saying anything to anyone, I'd made an appointment and been seen quite quickly by the midwife at our GP Surgery. I went to the first scan by myself because I wasn't sure how far along I was, and I wanted to surprise Hawk. Imagine my surprise when I found out I was over sixteen weeks. I knew my clothes had been getting tighter but figured it was because I couldn't seem to stop eating everything in sight. I guess that should have been my first clue.

Thanking the technician, I took the scans, popped them in my bag, and left the hospital. My first stop was the café where I picked up lunch for Hawk, me, and his receptionist. Yes, he'd finally found someone to man the front desk, and he'd also hired another tattoo artist. Neither of who had come via the usual channels. His receptionist had been brought by Ben, who had asked if Hawk could trial her for a month as she needed a break. Kelly was a sweet girl no older than eighteen who'd grown up rough. She had the scars to prove it, not just internal ones but external ones too.

His tattoo artist Raven had walked in one day with all his own equipment, handed Hawk a note and started setting up in one of the empty booths. Turns out he was a distant family member of one of the four giants that had rescued Kaleb. We knew a bit more about them now, not much, but a bit more.

Skinny had found out from an underground source that they were known as the Cursed Skulls. The last time they'd swept through the village, they'd each had a tattoo inked into them by Hawk depicting the name they were known as with a kickass skull.

They didn't wear anything to depict them as a

club, no insignia, nothing. Cahir had told Reaper for the work they did, they needed to be on the move and anonymous. Those they had helped each got a disc with their insignia stamped in and a way to contact them. They could pass it on or use it once only and only if they were genuinely in need. When I asked if we were going to get one, Silas had shook his head and explained that no, we wouldn't get one as family always had help. I must have looked confused because he'd looked at Cai, who'd sighed, bent down and popped out his dark contact lenses. When he'd looked up, I'd gasped because staring at me were the same green eyes I woke up to every morning, the same ones that a little boy that called me mummy had. Now that his eyes were green, I could see other resemblances – the black hair, the same chin, high cheekbones.

"What? How?" Hawk had muttered, stunned.

"It's a long story," Silas had said. "Not one we share, maybe one day, but not today. Just know you are doubly protected not just by your brothers but also by us."

We'd understood, and not long after that conversation, they'd left again. We hadn't seen them since, other than to have Raven turn up two months after they'd ridden away.

Most people did a double take when they saw Hawk and Raven standing together. They were often mistaken for brothers and had long ago stopped trying to explain that they were distant cousins; they looked enough alike that they could be brothers. The black hair, high cheekbones, and green eyes were a strong genetic link in all of them.

A few minutes later after leaving the cafe, I parked in front of the shop. Hawk was sitting at the reception desk, showing Kelly, his receptionist, something. I'd asked Mum to have Kaleb this afternoon.

Catching his eye as I got out of my car, I smiled wide at him before bending and picking up our lunch from the back seat. Closing and locking the car, I walked into the shop, stopping at the door that Hawk was holding open for me.

Titling my head up for the kiss I knew was coming as soon as he threaded his fingers into my hair. Letting me go with one last peck on my lips, saying softly, "Hi, Sweets, this is a nice surprise."

Holding up the bag, I explained, "I called Kelly and asked if you'd be free for lunch."

His eyes narrowed slightly as he looked at his shy receptionist, who squeaked but held her ground, nodding. "Yep, you're free. Your lunchtime client called and said he'd have to postpone. I booked him in for tomorrow's lunch instead."

Hawk folded his arms over his chest, "Really, because he never mentioned cancelling when I spoke to him yesterday."

Kelly's eyes flashed to mine as she shifted uncomfortably in her chair uttering a soft, "He had an unexpected emergency."

Taking pity on the poor girl, I slapped Hawk slightly on his stomach getting a grunt. "Leave Kelly alone, I asked her to book out your lunch because I needed to see you."

His attention snapped to me, "Why? What's wrong?"

I rolled my eyes at him, "Nothing's wrong, sheesh, can't I want to spend some uninterrupted time with you?" I said, walking towards Kelly, I put my hand in my bag and took out the lunch I got for her and Raven.

"Here you go, Kelly, thanks for organising this for me. Bon appétit. The grump and I will be in his office," I told her with a smile, before grabbing Hawk's hand and dragging him to his office. Not that he demurred, he happily followed me, "Are you checking out my arse, Hawk?"

"It's a fantastic arse, Avy. Of course, I am," he chuckled as we got to his office. Walking in, I gave a slight squeal as he pulled me to him, shutting the door and pushing me up against it before devouring my mouth.

His warm hands on my bare thighs lifting me up, pushing the material of my skirt out the way. Wrapping my legs around his waist, I rocked my hips against him, feeling the hard length of his cock bump up against my clit. With a gasp, I pulled back from his mouth and rocked faster against him. "That's right, Sweets, take what you need," Hawk instructed as he pulled the straps of my tank top and bra down, pressing small biting kisses to my exposed skin, shoving the cups of my bra down to get to my breasts he sucked an engorged nipple into his mouth. I was trying to be quiet, but it was hard, especially with how sensitive my breasts were. I slapped a hand to my mouth just as a cry escaped me as I came.

Hawk's hands were busy between us. Hooking my panties to the side, he filled me. Biting my lip, I tried to stop another cry from erupting from me. Opening my eyes, I stared into his lust filled green eyes and smiled, "Feels so good, Hawk, having you filling me."

Moving us away from the door to the more solid wall that wasn't going to bang as much as the door had been. He chuckled wickedly at me as he thrust up into me, "Yeah, Sweets, always feels good with you. Are you going to be quiet while I fuck you?"

"Probably not," I whispered against his lips, not caring who was out there, not when he was filling me up in the most delicious way. Taking my lips in a hard kiss, he pistoned his hips hard against mine, driving his cock into me time and again. I was close to coming a second time, whimpering slightly as the familiar wetness gushed from me. Hawk thrust a hand between us and pinched my clit, that was all it took for me to let go, wailing softly at the back of my throat as he drove his cock into me three more times before coming, his guttural groan muffled by my mouth. Opening my mouth, I stroked my tongue against his as he slowed his thrusts down until they were just little pulses. Letting him up for air, he pushed his head into my neck, pressing a kiss to my throat. Letting out a shuddering sigh of bliss, I ran my hand through his thick black hair.

"Love you, Avy, you're my everything," he said, pressing soft kisses on my throat.

My heart swelled with love at his words. He never said them lightly and didn't say them often, though he showed me and Kaleb all the time how much we meant to him.

"Love you too, handsome," I replied softly, resting my head against his. We stood there until clean up wasn't an option anymore, it was a necessity.

Once I was steady on my feet, I walked to the small bathroom that Hawk had attached to his office, thankful that I didn't have to do the walk of shame to the customer bathroom.

When I came out, Hawk was sitting on the couch and had unpacked lunch from the bag I'd dropped as soon as we walked in the door, and he'd pulled me into his arms. Luckily, it was just sandwiches, so we wouldn't need to re-heat anything.

Sitting down next to him, I snuggled closer to his side, patting the couch, "Is there a reason we didn't use this instead of the wall?" I chuckled, taking a bite of my sandwich, my eyes twinkling with laughter.

He grinned at me, brushing a strand of hair behind my ear, "Yeah, I didn't want to wait. It's a whole four steps away from the wall."

I laughed and rested my head against his shoulder as we ate our lunch, catching up about the different businesses and what was going on with everyone. While we lived in close proximity to each other, we all had separate lives, and the women of the MC did stuff separately from the men. Once we'd finished, I was tidying up our mess when Hawk asked me, "So, Sweets, other than catching up, was there another reason you came by?"

My eyes widened I'd nearly forgotten what I'd come to tell him. How did that happen? I was putting it down to being cock struck or maybe pregnancy brain was really a thing.

"Oh, fuck," I muttered, my cheeks heating slightly. Grabbing my bag, I pulled an envelope from out of its depths.

Taking a deep breath, I handed it to Hawk, rubbing my hands nervously down my thighs, although why I was nervous, I had no clue. I knew Hawk wanted more children, but this one was a bit of a surprise as I was still on the pill but apparently having strep throat and taking antibiotics cancelled out your pill. Who knew?

Opening the envelope, he pulled out the black and white scans. His entire body stilled as he looked at them, then at me, before looking back at the scans.

"Is this what I think it is?" he asked softly.

"Yes," I confirmed, nodding my head.

Hawk slipped off the couch, shoving the coffee table away, pushing my thighs apart enough so that he could fit between them as he knelt on the floor between my legs. Pushing my shirt up and pulling the waist of my skirt down to get to my exposed belly.

Bending, he pressed a gentle kiss to the hard swell. Lifting his head, he looked at me and there were tears in his eyes. I blinked hard at his next words, trying to hold back my emotions but knowing it was a wasted cause, "Thank you, Avy. After Rachel and Mike, I gave up, thinking that relationships weren't worth the pain. I pushed having a family out of my head. And then, there you were, waiting for me. And I knew then that what I'd had with her wasn't the real thing."

"The first time I saw you, I knew you were mine.

Spending time with you has always been one of my greatest pleasures. I couldn't wait to marry you so much so that I had to take control to ensure it happened. I love seeing you with my name on your cut even though the club voted it isn't needed. I love the fact that you don't seem to care that I need to mark you as mine so that every man knows you belong to me. Same as I proudly wear the badge saying I belong to you."

"Then Kaleb came into our lives, and you took him straight into your heart and loved him. Loved both him and me, even when I was being an arse struggling to accept him. You had enough faith in me to know I'd eventually get my head out of my arse. When he was taken, I thought it was my punishment for not loving him from the start."

"Oh, Hawk," I whispered softly, wiping a tear of his cheek, "you never said anything."

He shook his head, "No, because I was so angry at myself for not loving him from the start."

Cupping his face in my hands, I told him, "You were allowed to feel like you did. They betrayed you and Kaleb was the reminder, but I also knew that you'd come to love him because you have a big heart. You don't see it but the rest of us do."

Hawk closed his eyes, turning his head and pressing a kiss to my wrist, before opening them again, the love blazing from them had me catching my breath and any hope of holding onto my tears was lost when he continued, "I love you so much, Avs. I know I don't always say the words, but I want you to know that I love you with all that I am. And now. Now you're giving me something even more precious than I ever expected. Another person to love."

"Oh, Hawk," I cried out, bursting into tears, shoving my head into his shoulder, crying. I didn't say anything as he moved us around. When I finally stopped bawling my eyes out at his sweet words, he'd moved us both onto the couch with me sitting on his lap. Handing me a serviette that had come with our lunch, I dried my tears and blew my nose. Taking a deep breath, I tilted my head up and smiled tremulously up at him, proclaiming softly, "You complete me."

Hawk lowered his head to kiss me. We didn't leave his office for a long time, when we did, we found the shop had been locked and there was a note from Kelly on the door that she'd re-arranged all this evening's clients as she thought we could do with some time together.

I smiled when I read the note. Hawk just shook his head in amusement as we set the alarm, leaving the shop. I kept him on his bike in my rearview mirror all the way home.

Two weeks later, I took him with me for my next scan, and he cried again when we were told it was a girl.

When our baby girl was six months old, we again had tears running down our cheeks this time with laughter as we stared at the technician in disbelief, when she assured us that, yes, I was definitely four months pregnant and it was a boy.

"Holy fuck," Hawk whispered in disbelief, "we're going to have three babies under the age of five."

Snorting with laughter at the look on his face, the technician must have thought we were nuts by this point.

"Just as well we have a village," I pointed out.

His shoulders had slumped in relief at my words, "You're right," he stuttered out wiping tears of laughter from his eyes.

Imagine our surprise when five months later during labour when not one but two babies arrived. Our youngest daughter had been hiding behind her much bigger brother the whole time.

I guess it was too much for my husband because when I'd finally pushed the last baby out and looked for him, he was lying on the floor passed out.

I'd laughed hysterically and ordered a midwife to take a picture, which I'd promptly sent to the rest of the MC once I was feeling up to it.

He'd taken his ribbing good-naturedly. He was a fantastic dad, hands on with all our children. We stopped after four; I don't think either of us would have had any hair left if we'd had more.

Our easiest was Kaleb, he always had been, and I think he always would be. I loved that boy to the depths of my soul. All our children had the signature black hair and green eyes that were prevalent in Hawk's lineage. Our boys were both good looking, but oh my word, our girls ... our girls were gorgeous.

I had a feeling their teen years were going to be trying for their dad, brothers, and uncles.

I couldn't wait.

EPILOGUE
HAWK

Fifteen years later

We were dropping Kaleb off at a military base not too far from us for the start of his time in the army. I'd been sidetracked by an old team member and had been catching up explaining that we were here dropping my eldest son off.

Kaleb would be here for fourteen weeks doing the training that is required by all that enter our military.

Being at the base was bringing back lots of memories of when I'd first arrived for my training. Although I'd arrived with a lot less fanfare. We were garnering lots of attention as the whole MC had ridden to drop him off. Reaper still had contacts, and he'd gotten special permission to have us all here. How he did it I have no idea, but he did.

It was nearly time for us to go, and Kaleb had made the rounds saying goodbye to everyone.

His younger sisters and brother were over by the cars waiting to go. The girls had been crying, I could tell by the redness in their eyes. They were staring over to the right; I turned my head to see what they were looking at. What I found was my eldest son with his mum in his arms, holding her tight. He pressed a kiss to the top of her head as she cried in his arms. He was tall, taller than me. I guess he got his height from the giant relatives. He was a well-built boy; he'd started training from the age of five in the gym with Ben and Carly. I had no worries about him passing the physical side that he would be put through and he'd ace the hand-to-hand part.

Excusing myself, I walked over to where Kaleb and Avy were standing.

To hear him murmuring to her, "I'll be okay, Mum. I'll contact you when I can, okay."

She nodded her head against his chest and her eyes opened as I walked up to them. The agony in them nearly had me telling Kaleb that he couldn't stay, but we'd already asked him to wait until he was eighteen before joining, he could have joined at sixteen if he wanted.

Stepping up, I put a hand on the back of Avy's neck, threading my fingers through her hair, wrapping the other arm around Kaleb, pulling them both into my embrace.

"He'll be fine, Avy," I whispered against her hair. She nodded, her head still against his chest.

"I know, but he's my first baby."

I knew what she meant; he may not have come from either of us, and we didn't love our biological children any less than him, but there would always be that something a little special about the love we had for him.

I heard the call go out that we had to leave. Kaleb pressed a last kiss to Avy's head before passing her to Reaper, who had walked up to us when the call went out but not before telling her that he loved her.

Knowing Reaper would look after Avy while I said goodbye, I pulled Kaleb into a hard hug.

"Take care of yourself, son, and don't forget if you need us, you call us. We'll be here."

Nodding that he understood, he hugged me hard one more time, whispering softly, "Love you, Dad. Thank you for taking me in and loving me."

I closed my eyes against the tears that threatened and hugged him harder.

"It was no hardship, son; you were always ours."

Letting him go, I took Avy from Reaper and

pulled her into my arms. Kaleb was the last to walk away. We waited. He stopped at the top of the stairs leading into the building, turning he saluted as we'd practiced, tapped his fist to his heart, kissed his fingers and blew a kiss to us. Before turning and disappearing.

"Fuck," I whispered tightly, as Avy sobbed in my arms. Turning us, I walked us back to the cars, glad that I'd not ridden my bike. I'd wanted to spend as much as much time with Kaleb as I could.

Helping Avy into the car, I buckled her in and checked on our other three in the back seat. They were subdued, and the girls were silently crying. It wasn't just us that would miss him. Kaleb was a great big brother.

The brothers were on their bikes, waiting to leave. Walking around to the driver's side, I was just about to get in when one of my old army buddies stopped me.

"He'll be fine, Hawk. If he's anything like you, he'll thrive. Tell his mum I'll keep an eye out. I know what happened to him when he was a baby, we all do. It was all over the news, all of us that knew you were hoping that you would find him. Had a party when you got him back. Your MC has a lot of history in our ranks. I get that it's hard for her to see him leave. We'll keep him as safe as we can."

"Thanks," I said, clasping his hand and shaking it.

It took a lot to leave that day and the visits after were few and far between. Kaleb leaving left a big hole in our family, we all felt it.

But he loved being in the army. In fact, he thrived in the military. Taking after me he ended up training as a sniper. He stayed in for four years and he shone all that time. I often got updates from old friends still in the army about him, how he was a chip off the block, a great team member, easy to get on with, fiercely protective of his female counterparts. Every update I got made us prouder and prouder of him.

After the fourth year when it came time to re-enlist, he decided not to. He missed his family too much and decided that he'd hand in his twelve-month notice.

Avy had screamed out loud when he'd phoned to tell her his news. Her screaming had us running to find out what the hell was going on. A few tears were shed, knowing that we now had an end date that we could look forward to.

A calendar was drawn up, and we marked down the days until he was home with us.

The day he arrived back home was one for the memory books. There were a lot of tears, laughter, and a party in his honour.

It was strange to see him so grown up. I was proud of the man he'd become. He'd left us a boy, a serious boy, but still a boy, and while he was still serious, his eyes now held a darkness that hadn't been there when he'd left us. Thrilled that he was home, ready to make his place in the MC, whatever that may be.

That night in bed, in the darkness of the room that was our sanctuary from the chaos of our family, I whispered to Avy, "My heart is complete again." She hadn't asked what I meant because she knew. "Yeah," she whispered in agreement.

Rolling over, I settled between her thighs, kissing her long and deep, loving her as I always had and always would.

THE END

Acknowledgements

I would like to say a massive thank you to my Beta Reader Cloe Rowe lady you rock. I don't know what I would have done without you these last few years.

To all my beautiful fellow Indie Authors who have been absolute rockstars this year.

The support and love I've been given me this year has been phenomenal and I thank every single one of you.

To my husband for always encouraging me on whatever crazy idea takes me at the time. Being there for me, always putting me first and for treating me like a queen. After 29 years you are still my inspiration.

My eldest daughter Helen offered positive quotes and comments daily during this journey. I love you more than the whole world and don't know what I would do without you and your encouragement. Love you, baby.

To my youngest, my lovely Ria, I love your snarky comments when we have to share the same space while I write. Don't ever change. Love you to the moon and back.

To my mum, I honestly don't know what I would do without you. Love you.

To all my readers who took a chance on me with my first book Wild & Free and for reaching out with positive comments and suggestions.

One last thing .... REVIEWS feed an author's soul, and we learn and grow from them. Whether it be just a rating left or a few words they are what pushes us to keep writing.

Follow me:

Facebook – Michelle Dups

Instagram - author_michelle_dups

Goodreads - michelledups

Facebook Group - Chelle's Crows

Other Books by Author

Sanctuary Series

Sanctuary Book 1 – Wild and Free (Dex & Reggie)

Sanctuary Book 2 - Angel (Kyle & Lottie)

Sanctuary Book 3 – Julie (Julie & Joel)

Sanctuary Book 4 – Amy a Novella (Amy, Sean and Rory

Sanctuary Book 5 – The Russo's – TBA

Crow MC

Reaper

Onyx

Rogue

Draco

Dragon

A Crow Christmas

Avy

Noni - TBA

Navy - TBA

COMING 2024/2025

The O'Shea's

Saints Outlaws MC – Southampton Chapter

Second Generation of Crow MC